THE BETRAYAL OF EBONY MAKEPEACE

BRAD CULLEY MYSTERIES
BOOK 2

JANEEN ANN O'CONNELL

Copyright (C) 2022 Janeen Ann O'Connell

Layout design and Copyright (C) 2022 by Next Chapter

Published 2022 by Next Chapter

Edited by Lorna Read

Cover art by CoverMint

Mass Market Paperback Edition

This book is a work of fiction. Names, characters, places, and incidents are the product of the author's imagination or are used fictitiously. Any resemblance to actual events, locales, or persons, living or dead, is purely coincidental.

All rights reserved. No part of this book may be reproduced or transmitted in any form or by any means, electronic or mechanical, including photocopying, recording, or by any information storage and retrieval system, without the author's permission.

ACKNOWLEDGEMENTS

Without the support of my alpha reader, Denise Wood, this book would not have seen the light of day.

My beta readers — Ally Britnell and Debra Hammer — not only provided feedback on the plot, character development and let me know about typos, but they too are a great support.

To my publisher, Next Chapter Publishing and particularly its CEO Miika Hannila, I am very grateful for the opportunity to get my stories "out there".

Thank you for reading.

Janeen

CHAPTER A1

Note to readers

Hi there,

I am an Australian and as such, use the Australian (and English) spelling of words. If you are in a country that uses US spelling, please don't get cross with me because I spell differently.

Australia uses metric for measurement and distance. The characters talk in kilometres, not miles 😊

We have lots of little different quirks, even though we all technically speak the same language. Thank you for your understanding. I hope you enjoy the story.

Cheers
Janeen

CHAPTER B1

**In case you missed *Ebony Makepeace is Dead*, or it's been a while since you read it.
Here's a recap:**

Ebony Makepeace is an author who likes to eat cheese toasties and drink soy lattes in her favourite coffee shop in North Melbourne. One Tuesday morning in the café, while she has her head over her notebook, minding her own business and scribbling some ideas for her next novel, an odd-looking man, unknown to her, pulls out the empty chair at her table, and sits down. His attempts at trite conversation annoy her, and she hisses at him to go away. Instead, he bombards her brain with an unlikely story that someone wants her dead, and he is supposed to kill her. But, lucky for her, he is only going to wound her with the bullet he is about to release from the gun he is holding under the table.

Disbelief swallows Ebony's senses and not until she feels the searing pain in her side, does she realise what he said.

. . .

The Betrayal of Ebony Makepeace

While Ebony is in hospital recovering from the surgery to remove the bullet, the same man comes into her room, and injects something into the IV that is running into the cannula in her hand. Waking up cold and shaking, with a flimsy white sheet covering her, Ebony is confronted once again with the person she dubs Café Man. He explains he just saved her life by pretending she was dead. Now, she is to do exactly as he says.

Ebony's life as she knew it no longer exists. Her parents, her friends, her readers, her publisher, think she is dead. To protect her, Café Man moves her out of her North Melbourne apartment into his house overlooking Port Phillip Bay, at Altona. Like Café Man, who tells her his name is Bradley Hector Culley, Ebony does not know why she was a target for assassination. Although she feels like a prisoner, Brad does not treat her as one, and the more time she spends in his house, the more comfortable she feels with him. He only stays when he is invited, and a sketchy romance starts to develop.

Bradley works tirelessly looking after Ebony, making sure she is safe, creating a new identity for her (Sherryn Forbes) and appeasing his father, who ordered Ebony's death. Brad's best friend, police detective Ryan Sanderson helps facilitate Ebony's "murder" and "burial" and tries to keep his partner off Brad's trail.

. . .

Wearing an elaborate disguise, Ebony attends her own funeral and hears her mother speaking to a man who says he is Ebony's publisher. He introduces himself as Douglas Culley, owner of Sapphire Publishing. Ebony's world falls further into the chasm of chaos as she processes this information and shares it with Brad.

Brad tries to find a connection between his father publishing Ebony's books, and ordering her death.

Ebony Makepeace is dead, and Sherryn Forbes has taken her place.

1

BRAD

In what couldn't be worse timing, my phone rang as I negotiated the traffic congestion, which was, sadly, now part of my daily grind. A glance at the display on the dash showed it was my personal assistant, Ferdinand. I let it ring. Nothing he said to me would get me to the office any quicker. But he persisted, calling three more times before I answered.

'Were you asleep?' he asked sarcastically. 'While I am here running the show?'

'And you do a marvellous job running the show, Ferdie.' He hates being called Ferdie. But I pay him extremely well, so he can put up with my foibles now and again.

'The coroner has released your father's body. The funeral director wants you to call in, to see her — to plan the funeral.'

'You told her my calendar was free this morning, didn't you, Ferdie?'

'Of course I did. It is. Who else can do this last thing for your father? I told her you would be there around eight-thirty. See ya.'

Pangs of guilt at how my father died played with

anxiety in my gut. They had a wonderful time while I wrangled my emotions and the traffic. These days, I hated myself for having been so ready to blame him. I took his psycho behaviour at face value, eager for him to be the villain. Eager to point the finger at a soft target. My brother Steven was the true psycho. But my self-loathing changed nothing. I would organise a fitting farewell.

Ebony should have been with me to discuss arrangements, but I didn't want to turn the car around to go back and pick her up. Ebony and I lived in my place in Altona. Her decision. I preferred my townhouse in South Melbourne. Its location suited me: I could walk into the CBD of Melbourne if I felt so inclined, get to work quickly and, with easy access to Southbank, had my pick of great restaurants. But she liked the beach and had developed a fondness for a local café. And the local writing group she'd joined made her happy. After what my family put her through, it wouldn't kill me to suffer living by the beach.

The funeral director's premises were on a pleasant, tree-lined boulevard on the northern side of the city, where the tram line ran up the middle of the road. Further from the city than I would have liked. But Ferdinand, bless his heart, picked one that had a rainbow on its website. Externally, the building looked like a large Edwardian house. Inside, the ultra-modern, contemporary setting screamed wealth. I wondered how much wealth I'd be parting with.

Angela Blackwood was an impeccably presented

The Betrayal of Ebony Makepeace

older woman. She held out her hand and welcomed me, said she was pleased to make my acquaintance in such sad circumstances and showed me into her office. I thought my office was sumptuous; hers was next level. Two charcoal grey fabric couches that did not look shop bought — I made a mental note to ask her where she had them made — hugged the walls. Her large mahogany desk took centre stage. I noticed how tidy she had it, and a picture of my messy one flashed through my mind. Inoffensive artwork hung on the walls, which were painted a light grey; one of those colours that would take offence if you called it *grey*. It would see itself as Wooded Gum, or some other equally irrelevant name. The grey carpet appeared two or three shades darker than the walls, and they complemented each other well. An impressive space. Two armchairs that matched the couches sat on either side of a gas log fireplace. I hate pretend fires. This one, however, was the best I had seen, and I could almost smell the wood burning. She indicated I should sit in one of the chairs. Not as comfortable as it looked.

'Nice fire,' I said, no doubt impressing her with my wonderful command of the English language.

'Thank you. It's handy when we still get the odd cold day at this time of year. Spring is quite unpredictable, isn't it?'

I nodded. I didn't really want to engage in a conversation about the weather.

My phone vibrated in my pocket. I took it out, saw it was Ebony, and put it back without answering.

'Do you need to get that?' Ms Blackwood asked.

I shook my head. 'No. All good. Let's get on with the arrangements.'

Ms Blackwood ran a barrage of funeral *things* past me: the coffin, the type of service, the music, the video. She asked me who would speak, and who would be responsible for the eulogy. Would we have a presentation of my father's life? How many mourners did I think would attend?

I shrank into the uncomfortable armchair and wished the fire would swallow me up.

'Ms Blackwood, your attention to detail and your passion to do the best for the deceased is clear, but it is too much for me at the moment. My father's death is the tip of the iceberg. I've had a difficult year. My assistant Ferdinand will call you. He can handle the arrangements on my behalf.'

Ms Blackwood stood up, waited for me to do the same, and reached out to shake my hand. 'I completely understand, Mr Culley. There is a lot to consider. I'll wait to hear from your assistant.'

2

BRAD

Ebony wore a blonde wig, a grey hat that fitted perfectly, a soft pink cowl neck jumper, a black wool three quarter coat, dark grey trousers, and black shoes. She had a soft pink handbag over her arm. She looked awesome, and everyone turned to gawk at us when we walked into the chapel. No one who knew Ebony Makepeace would have recognised her. Sherryn Forbes was on my arm.

Mourners occupied every seat in the chapel. They left the front row for the family.

'I thought you said your father didn't have many fans,' Ebony whispered.

'This way, Mr Culley.' The funeral director's smile was sincere, not over the top. Kind, reassuring. She led Ebony and me to the front.

I considered my best friend Sandy to be family. His partner when he was in the police force, Tomy was, too. (Whenever she was introduced, she sounded out her name – *toe me.*) They sat in the second row. As we walked past, I told them to sit with us. Ferdinand also had a family position in the front. Before sitting down, I looked back at the people who had come to pay their respects. Two board members from the mining company my father ran were at the rear. Only two. I couldn't see my mother's brother, Uncle Walton, and made a mental note to find out why he wasn't there.

One of Sapphire Publishing's authors was Master of Ceremonies, and after the usual pleasantries, he launched into a spiel about how wonderful Douglas Culley had been: a great mentor and a genuine supporter of new talent. When he finished, he wiped his eyes, blew his nose, and stepped down. Three others from the publishing company my father used as a hobby, took turns to espouse the virtues of the man I called "Arsehole". Listening to the genuine appreciation and affection these people had for my father, I felt the guilt bubble away in my gut. My *family* handled the ordeal in their own way: Ebony fidgeted with the buttons on her jacket, Sandy bit his nails, Tomy's stare bore into the casket. Ferdinand checked his phone.

Ferdinand and Sandy stood with me in the chapel's foyer while I shook hands and thanked people for attending my father's funeral. Ebony kept out of the limelight, Tomy at her side. When refreshments appeared, people lost interest in me and wandered off to munch on sourdough sandwiches and an assortment of patisseries from the French bakery down the road. I acknowledged Ms Blackwood, indicated to Ebony with a flick of my head that she and Tomy should meet me outside, and walked with Sandy and Ferdinand to the car park.

'That was a surprise,' Tomy said, as we hovered around my vehicle.

'Tell me about it.' I leant back on the driver's door. 'Didn't I feel guilty when those people were singing his praises? Rhetorical question. I wish he had confided in me, had told me about my psychotic brother. We could have avoided all of this.'

'Maybe not,' Sandy mulled. 'Steven is very clever as well as mad. Not a good combination.'

'I should have killed him when my father told me to.'

I opened the car door and sank into the driver's seat. Ebony took up her position as front passenger, and Ferdinand sat in the back, fumbling with the seat belt.

'See you at Claude's Bar for dinner,' Sandy said, as he and Tomy got into his vehicle.

I didn't feel like going to the office, but pangs of responsibility, something I would have to learn to live with, stabbed at my head. Ferdinand had carried my accounting practice long enough. It was time I got back on track.

'I didn't expect you in the office today.'

Ferdinand's greeting had me looking over my shoulder to see who he was speaking to.

'You *are* talking to me! Why wouldn't I be here?'

'I thought you and Miss Forbes would console each other.' Ferdinand gave me the disapproving snarl he wore so well.

'There's work to be done, but don't let that stop you from criticising me.'

'That's rich. I'm the one who held this place together while you were missing.'

It annoyed me when my assistant made me feel as if I owed him. I did, of course, but I didn't need reminding.

'And who organised that beautiful service for my father?' Ferdinand always responded well to flattery.

'Well. Yes. That, too. Do you want me in your office?'

'When you're ready,' I challenged, opening my office door.

Ferdinand made himself comfortable in one of the leather armchairs, sitting back and arranging himself in a cross-legged position with a notebook on his knee.

'I am going to tell you some things you won't know. But it's important you understand what's been going on because I will need your help.'

He nodded his head. 'I'm listening.'

I sat in the chair opposite him and filled him in on the parts of the story surrounding my father's death that he didn't know. He didn't know about me being told to kill Steven. He didn't know Steven had refused to disappear and had been tormenting my father. He didn't know I had doubts my brother was telling the truth about my mother's death, or that I wondered if she really were dead.

Ferdinand took notes on his pad. The hieroglyphics were as foreign as if he were writing in Japanese. He took shorthand, a long-lost art, and to me the jottings on the page did indeed look like another language.

'Do we start with Steven's financial interests?' Ferdinand asked.

'We will look at those, but I think my mother's affairs should come first.'

3

EBONY

Ebony walked to her favourite café on Pier Street. Today was quiet. Mondays usually were. Tuesdays were busy because of the little street market along the footpath. Wednesdays were quiet in the colder months, but for the rest of the week she kept away from the thoroughfare unless she and Brad indulged in brunch. When she left the townhouse, she pulled her scarf up to cover her nose and mouth. Every now and then, the seaweed that washed up on the beach had a pungent smell which wafted all over the neighbourhood. Today was one of those days. It was the only thing about living here that she didn't like.

Brad, Sandy, and Tomy were Ebony's only friends in this life. Although she had two more friends in this life than she had in her previous one, she was often lonely. Going to the café filled a void.

The waiter acknowledged Ebony and followed her to the table with a jug of water in hand. He poured a glass and said he would be back with her flat white soy latte shortly. These little acknowledgements reminded her of her favourite café in North Melbourne;

the one where Brad shot her. She shivered at the memory.

Ebony smelt the freshly ground beans and her favourite soymilk brand long before the waiter put the coffee in front of her. She nodded and smiled at the young man when he asked if she would like to order her usual toasty.

While she waited for her lunch, Ebony organised her notebook and pencils and looked around the café and into the street for some inspiration. This book was not writing itself. Most of the others she'd written started with a sketchy plan and the characters took over quickly. They guided the plot and came up with problems for each other. She shook her head, wondering if being Sherryn Forbes and not Ebony Makepeace was affecting her mojo.

The vibration and buzzing of her phone as it danced around inside her bag startled her. She looked at the screen. Brad.

'Hi there,' she said, swallowing a mouthful of coffee.

'Hi. I'll be late tonight. Ferdinand and I are working through a search, and I'm going to visit my mother's family estate before I come home.'

'Oh. Ok. But it's your turn to cook.' Ebony would not let Brad weasel out of the agreement he'd made with her. She was determined not to be the "housewife".

'Fair enough. Don't want to appear as if I'm manipulating our arrangement. I'll go tomorrow. I'll be home at the usual time. Love you.'

'Bye,' Ebony said without returning Brad's "love you." She knew that would annoy him and grinned when she held the coffee cup to her mouth.

The cheese toasty arrived, and Ebony asked for another coffee. As the young man sauntered away, he jumped from the tiled floor of the café to her notebook. He would be her protagonist.

Ebony scrawled notes while she drank coffee and munched on her sandwich. Sherryn Forbes was writing at last.

With her mojo back and sandwich finished, Ebony picked up her things, paid for her lunch, and stepped out onto Pier Street. She cast a casual glance through the window of the café as she walked past. There, large as life, chatting to a man, was Sophie Marris, Ebony's editor at Sapphire Publishing. She told herself she was Sherryn Forbes, and that her disguise was fantastic, but that didn't stop a bubble of fear rising in her chest.

4

BRAD

I left Ferdinand to plough through my mother's financial history, with instructions to note anything out of the ordinary. In his usual turbulent style, he demanded to know what I considered out of the ordinary. I couldn't say, so told him to use his imagination. 'You are an auditor, after all.' I heard his grumbles when I pushed the button to call the elevator.

Just what I expected to find at my mother's family estate in Macedon was a mystery. I hadn't been there since she "died". Her brother, who was executor of her will, and lived there, had been difficult to reach, and kept his cards close to his chest.

I pushed the button on the pillar that held up the steel gates and waited. The sprawling Macedon property had been in Mother's family since the 1880s. Her brother, Walton – yes, that's his first name – never married and had no children. He lived in the expansive mansion with enough staff to fill a small church.

A solicitor, he had worked from here forever. Long before the pandemic, when working from home became the "norm".

'Yes?' asked a voice that sounded like a member of the Royal household had popped in for a visit.

'It's Bradley Culley. I'd like to see my uncle, please.'

'Mr Warburton is not taking visitors. He is working.'

Every time I thought of my uncle's full name, I wanted to either spew or screech hysterically — Walton Warburton — not pretentious, much. Mother had called him Wally.

'I've left messages. He is not returning my calls. It is imperative that I speak with him.'

'You need an appointment.'

'Then make me one, for fuck's sake.'

The speaker fell into a deafening silence. 'Temper, temper,' I chastised myself. The hoity, hoity toity at the other end of the two-way wouldn't have appreciated my language.

'Hello? I apologise.' My eyes rolled at the windscreen. 'I'm sorry for my language. We buried my father on Friday. I am still a bit on edge.' I gripped the steering wheel while I waited to hear if my grovelling worked.

'Very well. I am sorry for your loss.'

God, I hate that term, *sorry for your loss*, it's so insincere. I waited.

'Mr Warburton will meet with you for twenty minutes at eight-thirty tomorrow morning.'

That was it. Nothing else. Silence. I reversed the car out of the driveway and began the one-hour journey back to Melbourne.

Ferdinand's voice broke the monotony that was the Calder Freeway. 'I have found nothing unusual.'

'Thank you. We'll keep looking. Go home and I'll see you later tomorrow morning.' I explained to Ferdinand about my uncle granting me permission to see him the next day.

'By the way, Miss Forbes called. She didn't sound impressed when I said you had gone to Macedon. See you tomorrow.'

More explaining to do.

———

I pulled into the garage of the Altona house and took the groceries out of the back. I hated it when it was my turn to cook, which happened every other night. Because of my poor culinary repertoire, I always cheated. Ebony, if annoyed, didn't let on. Bless her. Tonight, the menu choice of pasta (my reliable fallback when I had given little thought to what we were eating) would win me points. I bought plant-based *meatballs* at the supermarket — because she is still a vegetarian — and two jars of expensive pasta sauce that had cherry tomatoes and parmesan cheese in it. I didn't mind the plant-based stuff. If you smothered it with an interesting sauce, it was edible.

Ebony accosted me as soon as I walked into the kitchen. 'I called you today. You didn't answer. I rang Ferdinand, and he said you went to Macedon. You said you weren't going.'

'Hello, dear. It's lovely to see you too.' I dumped the groceries on the bench. 'I went early afternoon so I could be back to cook dinner.'

'What are we having?'

'Pasta.'

'Ok. Put the water on to boil, I have something to tell you.'

The dramas in our lives had not ended after the death of my father. When Ebony said she had something to tell me, it usually meant a headache was around the corner.

I put water in one large saucepan, added a pinch of salt, put on the lid, and turned on the hotplate. Ebony opened the jars of sauce, tipped them in a deep frypan with the pretend *meatballs*, and put the lid on that one. All sorted. She poured us both a glass of red, and we sat opposite each other in the family room.

'What has happened?' I coaxed.

'I had lunch at the café today and did some writing.'

'Excell...' She held up her hand to stop me from speaking. When she did things like that it reminded me of one of my teachers in primary school. *I wonder if dressing up in a school uniform is something she would consider in the bedroom?*

'Are you listening?' Ebony's voice stormed into my daydream.

'Of course I am.' I sipped the wine.

'As I was leaving the café today, I glimpsed a face I knew. I looked for a second to be sure.

'Were you?' I asked unnecessarily. This revelation would come in the story's telling. She was, after all, a writer.

She huffed. 'Yes, Brad, I am sure. It was Sophie Marris.'

I took another sip of wine, which seemed to annoy her. I sat there, not knowing what to do or say.

'The water's boiling,' she growled.

I put the glass down, hurried to the stove, threw a couple of handfuls of pasta into the pot, put the lid back on, turned down the hotplate, and walked back over to the couch. 'Is that when you called me?'

'Yes,' she snapped. 'I called you while I was walking home. You didn't answer.'

I took the phone out of my pocket, scrolled through the call log, and saw a missed call from her. 'I must have been out of signal range.' I let the comment about her walking home float on the surface of unresolved moments. It was good to hear her say *home*.

'I'll explain about Macedon later,' I said, going over to stir the pasta and the sauce. 'What do we make of Sophie Marris being in a café in Altona?'

Ebony shrugged. 'I was glad I'd worn my disguise.'

I paced up and down the kitchen. It gave me a chance to think, and to keep an eye on the pasta in case it boiled over.

'Was she with anyone?' I finally asked.

'Yes. No one I recognised.'

'Could just be a coincidence,' I said, trying to get my brain to process the information coherently.

'Could be. We've never met in person. I only have the profile on my...' Ebony paused, 'on your father's publishing company website to go by. And she only had my publicity shots.'

'Hopefully, the disguise worked.' I stirred the pasta, drained it, and spooned it into the pan that had the awesome smelling sauce and *meatballs*.

'I'll set the table,' Ebony said.

We ate our dinner in silence. Neither of us could work out why Sophie Marris was in Altona, and why in the café Ebony frequented.

'Do you think it's something we should be worried about?' she asked, taking our plates to the kitchen sink.

'Well, at least be on guard. I'm not sure it's a coincidence. I'll call Sandy first thing. There's nothing we can do now.'

'Perhaps if you'd answered your phone when I called, I wouldn't be going to bed worried.'

'Let me do the worrying, Ebony,' I soothed. 'Let's talk about my visit to my uncle's place in Macedon.'

'Why did you go?' she asked.

'To make a start on the investigation of Mother's death, or disappearance. I'm not sure which. I've been trying to reach my uncle ever since Steven took off. He ignores me so I drove up there.'

'You haven't told me about your mother's family.' She tilted her head to the side like a puppy, waiting for a response.

When I told her my uncle's name, Ebony put her hand over her mouth, trying to cover up the laugh that made its way out into the world, despite her efforts to keep it buried.

'Oh, you're serious,' she giggled. 'What was your mother's name? You've never told me. Something as funny as her brother's?'

'Wilhelmina.'

I'm sure the neighbours on the other side of the concrete wall that separated the townhouses heard her guffawing.

'Wilhelmina and Walton Warburton. What were your grandparents thinking? What were their names?'

'It doesn't matter.' I started loading the dishwasher.

She came around and put her arms about my chest while I rinsed the pan. 'I liked that sauce, and the plant-based *meatballs* were delicious.' She kissed me on the cheek. 'I'm going upstairs.'

I trundled up after her, hoping she had issued an invitation.

5

BRAD

This trip up the Calder Freeway annoyed me. If Wally the Wanker had only answered my calls, or seen me yesterday, I wouldn't be wasting my time. The freeway's surface was mostly good, but it wound its way through boring pine tree plantations and the proverbial Australian bush. The monotony was only broken with exit signs to out-of-the-way country towns and the carcasses of kangaroos who, during the night, played chicken with the traffic. The authorities cleared roadkill from highways like this one, but on the not-so-main roads, they left the dead wildlife for the ravens. Big red crosses were spray-painted on their bodies to show they had been checked for joeys.

I pressed the call button and waited for the servant, or butler, or bodyguard, or gardener, or whoever the bloody hell was running the show, to acknowledge me.

The gates opened without so much as a *good morning*.

The circular driveway had been paved since the last time I drove through the gates, which was nearly two years ago. It wasn't just ordinary concrete, it was the speckled stuff, in a grey that matched the bricks on the house. Must be good money in the law. I pulled up at the front steps, got out, and pressed the remote to lock the car.

'No need to lock the car, sir.' A fair-haired, good-looking man in a pale blue polo shirt and navy blue trousers stood on the front step. He owned the voice that was *sorry for my loss* yesterday.

'Habit,' I grumbled. Wanting to add that he should mind his own business.

'Please follow me.'

Polo Shirt led me to my uncle's office. He wasn't there.

'I'm on time,' I complained. 'He's allocated me twenty minutes.' Sulking, I made my way to the leather couch that ran along the wall opposite a bookcase. I tapped my watch and glared at Polo Shirt. 'Time's tickin'.'

Walton Warburton sauntered into the room as if he were a member of the Royal Family. 'Sorry to keep you, Bradley,' he sneered. Bastard had heard me grumbling.

I stood and offered my hand, which he shook, before moving to his desk and squirting hand sanitizer onto his palms.

'Throwback to the pandemic. A good habit to continue, I feel.'

I stared at him. He'd put on at least ten kilos since I'd seen him last. The lines on his face looked like an old roadmap and large dark circles rested under his eyes. 'You look well, Uncle,' I lied.

'No. I don't. You do, though. What did you want to see me about?'

'I don't have time in less than twenty minutes to explain everything, but I want to ask this: do you believe Mum is really dead?'

He looked genuinely perplexed. 'Why?'

'Turns out my brother is a psychopath or sociopath, or whatever the correct term is. I have a niggling suspicion he had something to do with Mum's death or disappearance.'

'There was a funeral.' My uncle frowned, confusion burying itself into the wrinkles. 'I've almost finalised her estate. You and your brother get a substantial amount, I might add, now that your father is deceased.'

I wanted to ask how much, but thought it unseemly. I looked at my watch. 'There aren't many of our twenty minutes left.'

'Don't worry. My first appointment isn't until ten. Phillip likes to coddle me. Tell me about Steven and why you have questions about your mother's death.'

I kept the explanation brief and to the point. I didn't tell him about Ebony, but shared the story about my saving Steven, and how he was manipulating our father, and how he disappeared when they released him on bail, after being charged with kidnapping and assaulting me.

'Oh dear. Are you alright now? It's dreadful that Douglas felt trapped. I always liked him. The family was happy Mina married someone with their own wealth. I don't understand why you are asking if she is dead, though.'

I didn't answer his question about whether I was ok. It lost its importance. 'I think my brother had something to do with her *death*. She was in very good health, she was happy, had come to terms with my father's long work hours, and built a life she enjoyed. We ate together once a week. There was no reason for her to die.'

'A friend of mine was having dinner with his mother one night. The woman was in her late forties, healthy, fit. She had a brain aneurism at the table and dropped dead there and then.'

'Mum didn't drop dead at the table. Steven said she died in her sleep. I haven't seen the autopsy report. Can you get it for me, Uncle Walton?'

'Your father would have a copy.'

'I don't want to go through my father's things looking for it. You're a solicitor, and her brother. They'll give it to you won't they?'

'In non-suspicious deaths, the reports are digitised, Brad. It will be online.'

Uncle Walton stood up, moved around in front of his desk, and gave me a hug. The hand sanitizer would have a big job once I'd left. 'I'll see what I can do. I'll be in touch.'

'Before I leave, Uncle, why did you not attend my father's funeral?'

'I did, Brad. I left as the coffin was being taken to the hearse. I felt uncomfortable. I had made no attempt to see your father since Mina died. Guess I felt a bit guilty.'

'Guilt is a feeling I have to learn to live with, too.'

Polo Shirt showed me out the front door. He reminded me a bit of the goons my father used to have watching his and my every move at his office. Creepy. All-knowing.

The Betrayal of Ebony Makepeace

Ferdinand was making a latte for my eleven o'clock appointment when I stepped off the elevator and walked into the office. 'Just in time,' he snapped.

'Good morning, Ferdie,'.

He bristled. 'Mr Robert Fielding is waiting in your office. You do remember the names of your clients, don't you?'

'I don't have to, Ferdie. I have you.'

Mr Fielding was sitting on the Chesterfield that hugged one side of the room, and stood when I walked in. I manage and move around a lot of money for him, and he pays me handsomely for my efficiency. He adds a little extra because I am discreet.

'I am very sorry to hear about your father's death, Brad.'

'Thank you.' Before the pandemic, we would have shaken hands in greeting. Neither of us were into the elbow bump, so words sufficed.

'I didn't know him, but knew of him. His publishing business was highly regarded in the industry.'

'So I discovered at his funeral,' I said.

'You didn't know?' Confusion etched into the frown on his forehead.

'I did not know he had a publishing business until Ebony...' My mouth closed before I finished the sentence.

'I see,' Fielding mumbled into his coffee cup, before putting it down on a side table without using a coaster. 'Then you might be surprised when you discover why I am here today.'

He opened his briefcase and took out a memory stick.

'I've expressed an interest in another business. I'm

led to believe it is going up for sale as soon as they grant probate. I would like you to check the books. This USB has all the information on it.'

He handed it to me.

'The business is called Sapphire Publishing.'

6

SANDY

Ryan Sanderson swiped his mobile's screen to answer the call before he looked to see who it was. 'Detective Sergeant Sanderson.'

'What? Who?'

'It's taking me a while. Be gentle.'

'Chosen an office space yet? And when you were a cop, you didn't use your whole fancy title.' Brad Culley moved the phone away while he coughed.

'I'm confused. Have you got COVID?'

'That's so last year. No, I don't. Answer my question.'

'Yes. It's a great location and a really good set-up. I'm here now.'

'You're welcome.'

'Give a man a chance. Anyway, all you did was introduce me to the real estate agent, tell her what I wanted, and where, and how much I was prepared to pay.' Sandy could imagine Brad shaking his head in mock disbelief.

'When can I come and see you? I want to pick your brain.'

'Hang on, let me check my diary.'

Brad laughed until he started coughing again.

'You should see a doctor.'

'Whatever. I'm on my way.' Brad Culley disconnected the call before Sandy could object.

'You'll have to rush off to that cheap furniture place to get set up before you see clients,' Brad said, stepping into his friend's new office space. 'It's airy and bright, at least. Has a good view. Have you thought of a business name yet?'

'Ryan Sanderson Investigations.' The grin spread across Sandy's face.

'You're not serious. Sandy, Sandy, Sandy. Call Ferdinand and make an appointment with me. We'll work out a catchy name, set up your business accounts and order some stationery. You must look the part. And right now, you look like one of Homer Simpson's mates at the nuclear power plant.'

'Nice. Good friend. Thanks. You wanted to see me about something? Pull up a chair.'

Both men sat cross-legged on the floor, sipping the iced coffee Brad had arrived with.

'Sophie Marris was in the café Ebony frequents on Pier Street.'

'When?'

'The other day. Ebony was leaving and saw her out of the corner of her eye. She was talking to a man Ebony didn't know. She said Sophie didn't notice her.'

Sandy wriggled and tried to make himself more comfortable. Disquiet settled in the pit of his stomach. 'There's something I gleaned from the interview with the goons that babysat your father, that I didn't tell you.' Sandy put his coffee down on the beautifully polished timber floor and waited while Brad did the same.

'What?'

'Steven was sleeping with Sophie.'

Brad unravelled his legs and stood up. He glared down at his friend. 'How could you have kept that from me?'

'I forgot. We had plenty on our plates as it was. I thought Steven had used Sophie to find out the information. I didn't think it was ongoing or serious.'

'This creates more anxiety and insecurity. I can't tell Ebony.' Brad started pacing around the room.

Sandy stood up and moved the coffee cups to the windowsill. 'I'm sorry, Brad.'

'Hmm. Tell me everything. Don't leave anything out.'

'There's nothing more to tell. One goon said it while they were leaving, as an *Oh, by the way*.'

'Some *by the way*. Where is she working now? I want to talk to her.'

'That's not a good idea. I'll investigate. It can be my first job.'

Brad walked to the window. 'Which coffee is mine?'

Sandy searched on his phone for nearby furniture stores, sending details of two stores he liked the look of to his planner. He toyed with a colour scheme and style in his head while walking to his car. The distraction didn't last long, and before he turned on the ignition, he had played the revelation by the goons, of

Sophie Marris and Steven Culley's dalliance, over and over again to make sure he hadn't missed anything. He called Tomy.

'Hi, my no longer police detective friend.' Tomy sounded cheerful. Not her usual mindset.

'I've got an office now. Brad said I have to think up a name for the business. He doesn't like the one I decided on.'

'I don't know what it is, but knowing you, it would be boring as hell.'

'There you are. I wondered where you went.'

'Hilarious. I'm trying to be a new me.'

'It isn't working. Do you have a few minutes to see me? I want to listen to the recording I took when I spoke to Steven Culley's offsiders. Particularly the part where they told me Steven was sleeping with Sophie Marris.'

'You didn't tell me they said that.'

'Don't get cranky with me. Brad is furious I didn't tell him at the time, too. He seems to have forgotten he was tied up and being tortured. It wasn't deliberate, not telling you. My mind pushed it aside until just now.'

―――

Tomy had the memory stick already in her computer when Sandy finally got clearance to go into the building and to her office.

'Didn't take them long to treat me as an outsider,' Sandy grumbled as he pulled up a chair to sit next to his ex-partner.

'Stop complaining. You didn't have to resign. How far into the recording was this bombshell dropped?'

'It was as they were leaving. One of them turned around and told me. I wonder if he kept it till last deliberately?'

Tomy opened the file containing the recording, and fast-forwarded to about ten minutes before the end.

When Steven found out about Miss Makepeace's book—he was sleeping with Sophie Marris by the way—he decided Ebony had to go. Brad was the ideal assassin: obedient, loyal, trustworthy. Mr Culley was given his orders and Brad stalked his victim. But just as he couldn't kill his brother, he couldn't kill Miss Makepeace.'

'Wait. What do you mean, he couldn't kill Miss Makepeace?'

'Seriously, detective. We are professional investigators among several other things. We picked up the signs. Brad did a good job until he moved Miss Makepeace into his house in Altona. But Douglas Culley thought she was dead. We told Steven she wasn't, but he lost interest in her when her life fell apart and she had to run. But he wanted her notebooks and would do anything to get them.'

Tomy clicked the stop icon on the recording. 'The plot thickens.'

'It gets even thicker.' Sandy squirmed in the chair. 'Brad said Sophie Marris was sitting in the café Ebony goes to every couple of days. She was with someone else who Ebony didn't recognise. I told Brad this could be my first case.'

'Do you think she was with Steven Culley?'

'I don't know. Possibly.'

'Well, if you find out it was him, you must, must, must, tell me. Him being missing is a police matter, not a private investigator one.'

'Can you email that little piece of recording? Please.'

'I can. But will I? That is the question.' Tomy closed the recording program on the computer, and took out the memory stick. 'I'll see.'

'Times have certainly changed. Catch you soon, Tomy.' Sandy put the chair back behind the desk on the other side of Tomy's and made his way to his car. *I'll have to get furniture for the office organised. I think this case will keep me busy.*

7
BRAD

I received hundreds of emails a day. Ferdinand vetted them and forwarded the ones he thought I should handle. I was in the middle of looking over the books of Sapphire Publishing when the tell-tale beep interrupted my train of thought. Clicking on the email program, I saw my uncle's name at the top of the list.

Good morning, Brad, I hope this finds you well. (Whatever.)
I have attached the autopsy report for you. It is online. The cause of Mina's death was a brain aneurism. You will see when you read it that there were no suspicious circumstances noted.
I will finalise her estate, but won't distribute the funds until we find out what is happening with your brother. The money will stay in the Estate of Wilhelmina Culley. But please let me know if you are not happy with this arrangement.
Cheers
Uncle Walton.

That was the end of me for an hour. I brooded,

fretted, and scowled through the autopsy report, and my uncle's email. The nail in the coffin, so to speak, was having to go over the books of my father's publishing company. I didn't summon Ferdinand. He didn't need to see another one of my hissy fits. From what I understood, my parents both had Uncle Walton do their wills, and as he was executor of Mum's, why not Father's?

I pushed my chair back from my desk and walked around for a while. My head pounded. The new pieces of information swirled around, trying to settle, trying to find a place where they belonged. So many new dramas. I hate drama.

Speaking of drama, Ferdinand opened the door and strolled in. 'Are you ok?'

'Why?'

'The walls are opaque glass, Brad. I can see you pacing up and down. I can see the stress sprouting from your head.'

'Did you read the email from my uncle?'

'The one marked "private and confidential"? Of course I did.'

I couldn't manage my life or my business without Ferdinand. But sometimes I could throw him in front of a bus. 'So you understand why I'm agitated.' I stopped pacing and glared at him.

'Not really. Seems straightforward to me. What are your plans?'

'I don't know.' I moved back behind my desk and waved at Ferdinand to leave my office. He bowed as if I were a deity, and walked backwards through the door.

My uncle didn't say to contact him, but I dialled his number, anyway. He didn't answer. I left a brief message saying I'd read the email, and I thought we should chat. Then I called Sandy.

'I've got some nice furniture for the office,' he said into the phone, as soon as he accepted the call.

'That's lovely for you, dear,' I mocked. 'Meet me at Claude's tonight.' I hung up. If it didn't suit Sandy to meet me, he would text. No need to tell him a time. We always met at seven.

As usual, I arrived before him. It beggars belief that now he is self-employed and not at the behest of the police department, he still can't be on time.

The waiter wandered over and asked if I would be having dinner. I hadn't thought of that and suddenly remembered Ebony. 'I'll wait until my friend gets here,' I stuttered. 'I'll have a flat white while I wait, please.' He nodded and strolled away as casually as he had arrived.

I took out my phone and called Ebony.

'You are not going to be late, are you?' she growled before I spoke.

'Yes. I am. I'm sorry I didn't call earlier; it's been a difficult day.'

'You're at Claude's. I can hear the background noise. Your day can't have been that bad if you are hunkered down in a bar.'

Sometimes being in a relationship was hard work, and since Ebony had come to terms with being Sherryn Forbes, I swear she was more cantankerous. 'I'm sorry, Eb. I'll fill you in when I get home. It's about my mother's death. See you later, Sandy has just walked in.' I hung up before she could complain or whinge or whine about why I was with Sandy and not her.

'Trouble in paradise?' Sandy pulled out his chair and plonked down on it.

'At least I have a paradise,' I mumbled.

'That's not nice. I don't have time for a relationship. And by the sounds of things, neither do you.'

He was right.

'Do you want dinner?' I asked, as the waiter began his wander over to our table.

'Sure. That would be good.'

The waiter put my coffee on the table, tapped our orders into his tablet, and scurried off.

'What's wrong?' Sandy led with the interrogation.

'My uncle got the autopsy report on my mother's death. The finding was *brain aneurism*. How can a perfectly healthy woman in her early fifties have a brain aneurism when there is no history?'

'Didn't you or your father see the autopsy report?' Sandy asked.

'I didn't know there was one, and thought nothing of it.'

'Well, someone in the family has a copy. So if it wasn't you or your uncle, then it was your father or Steven.' Sandy scanned the room, moving his eyes from one side of the space to the other.

'What are you looking at?'

'I'm hungry.'

'Of course you are. Could I have your undivided attention until you start filling your face?'

Sandy nodded, still glancing around intermittently.

'You're not going to starve for fuck's sake.'

The Betrayal of Ebony Makepeace

'I'm sorry. I am listening. What else did your uncle say in his email?'

'Nothing. He's keeping the money from Mum's estate in a trust account until we find out what is going on with Steven. Reading between the lines, he seems suspicious of Steven.'

Our meals placed in front of us, we continued speaking between mouthfuls.

'Your mother was cremated, wasn't she?'

'Steven organised it. I remember Mum saying once when we went to one of her aunt's funerals that she wanted to be buried. She and Father even had their plots selected and paid for. Steven put her ashes in the plot. I thought at the time it was a waste of money and space.'

'He's a clever operator, your brother. Once the autopsy report established the cause of death and no red flags were raised, he could move quickly.'

'To do what?'

'Take money, belongings, control of your father.'

I suddenly lost my appetite and put my knife and fork in the "finished eating" position and pushed my plate away.

'Not finishing it?' Sandy asked, hunger lighting up his face.

I shook my head, and the plate magically found its way to Sandy's side of the table.

8

Walton Warburton read over his email for the third time before clicking the send icon. He wanted to make sure the information he sent to Bradley was accurate and clear. Until his nephew visited, he had thought little about the circumstances of his sister's death, even though she was younger than him. These things happened. Now his assessment of events after her death required a rethink.

He pushed his chair back away from his desk and forced his arthritic knee to straighten. The surgeon recommended waiting before he had a knee replacement. 'They only last fifteen years,' he'd said. 'You'll need another one before you die.' With the stabbing pain enveloping his kneecap and the surrounding tendons and cartilage, Walton wondered how sensible the doctor's counsel was. He paced around the room, trying to get his right knee to bend a little without exacerbating the pain. Leaning his hands against the mantlepiece and bending over slightly relieved some of the pressure. Just as movement returned to the frozen knee, Phillip knocked on the office door saying Walton's client was waiting in the library.

The Betrayal of Ebony Makepeace

Walton limped back to his desk and put the printed version of his sister's autopsy report in the top drawer. He didn't sit back down until his client was comfortable.

———

Brad's name came up on Walton's phone just as he'd poured his after dinner port. 'Hello, Brad.'

'Good evening, Uncle. I'm sorry to call so late. Are you up?'

'Jesus, Brad, I'm in my early sixties, I'm not 109. Yes, I'm up.'

Walton didn't hear an apology from his nephew, but it was clear in his tone. 'I had dinner with my friend Sandy. He was a police detective until the fiasco that was Steven's legacy.'

'Go on.'

'He said we should be concerned about Steven's relatively quick organisation of Mum's cremation.'

'I'm angry with myself,' Walton said, between sips of port. 'I should have spoken up at the time. Mina wanted to be buried. She was always adamant about that. But I thought your father might not appreciate the interference.'

'Life is full of *if only*, Uncle. My head hurts when I go through all the *if only*'s I've accumulated lately.'

'What now?'

Walton listened as his nephew relayed his dinner conversation with his friend Sandy, his friend's opinions and recommendations and their next steps.

'Don't rely on me too much, Brad. I will help wherever I can with resources and legal expertise, but I am busy with my practice, so can't devote days on end to your investigation.'

Disappointment seeped from Brad's voice. 'I understand. My practice suffered when Steven was busy manipulating us all. I'll keep you up to speed and you can let me know when you're available.'

Walton and his nephew hung up simultaneously, and he poured himself another glass of port, hoping the warmth of the alcohol would soften the pain that would come from his knee when he stood.

The property Walton and his sister inherited from their parents was left in his care. Wilhelmina made quarterly contributions to its upkeep and often stayed when her boys were small, but Walton never moved out. He lived in the eight bedroom, five bathroom house while his parents were alive, and stayed on after their deaths. The conversation with Brad kept him awake, defeating the port in the race to unconsciousness.

At first light, he checked his diary to see if he had time, then sat down at his desk to draft a new Will. He inherited his sister's share of the estate when she died, but had never thought of it as belonging to anyone but himself. It was time to consider the future of the family estate.

Walton's assistant, come confidant, come friend, Phillip, knocked on the study door, did not wait for a response, and brought in a tray of Vegemite toast, orange juice, and a latte.

'Are you ok?' Phillip asked.

'Didn't sleep well. Had a phone call from Brad last

night and our chat kept me awake. Made me think about this place and what could happen to it when I die. I've got to work some things out. When is my first client?'

'Not until this afternoon. I left this morning free to give you a break. It seems the entire city is buying and selling real estate. I don't want you to get bored working on the same stuff. This afternoon's appointment is for estate planning. Appropriate in the circumstances.'

Walton nodded, and Phillip closed the door on his way out.

Logging on to his laptop, Walton started the spreadsheet program and typed in the names of the people he would like to look after, in his Will. At the top of the list was Phillip. The man had been with Walton for twenty years, having started when the legal practice was in its infancy. He would include Bradley, but hesitated before typing in *Steven*. If he didn't include Steven, although he knew little of the man, he suspected he would tie up the funds in legal battles until there was nothing left for his brother.

Phillip brought in morning tea: coffee, a blueberry muffin (warm) and a banana. 'Stop for twenty minutes. It will still be there when you've finished your break.'

'Join me,' Walton said standing up from his desk and moving to the couch on the other side of the room.

'There are two cups on the tray,' Phillip said, picking one up. 'The muffin and banana are for you. I had something before. Your limp is bad today. Why?'

'My knee. It freezes if I sit down with it bent for too long. And I keep forgetting to straighten it.'

'Do you want me to make an appointment with the specialist?'

'No. If you could get the exercise bike out of the garage and put it in the bedroom next to mine, I'll start riding that a little each day. I read somewhere that exercise bikes help. I'll try it."

The two friends slipped into a comfortable silence.

'I'll have the cook set up lunch on the verandah so you can enjoy the sunshine. Summer's relentless heat and hot north winds are not far away.'

'I'm not a fan of summer,' Walton said, putting his empty cup on the tray.

'I know.'

Left alone, Walton made the finishing touches to his Will. Using clear wording to avoid misinterpretation, he laid out his wishes: Brad and Steven would inherit the estate, and a substantial amount of Walton's cash-at-hand would be set aside for the ongoing maintenance of the property. He knew he could not make a legally binding caveat that prevented the sale of the estate, but made a note that he wished it to stay in the family. Steven and Brad would share equally in twenty-five percent of the cash and shares Walton possessed, Phillip would have twenty-five percent, twenty-five percent to Animals Australia, and the remaining twenty-five percent to be shared equally between those members of staff who had been in his employ for five years or more. (There were four.)

Walton clicked the print icon and put the three-page Will on his desk. His client could witness his signature.

9

SANDY

Sandy made his way to Brad's office. He hated going there. Ferdinand didn't hide his disdain for him, and it made him uncomfortable. Brad seemed oblivious to Ferdinand's attitude.

'Oh, it's you. I forgot you were coming. Sit down over there, please.'

Sandy followed Ferdinand's instructions without commenting. He sat, playing with his phone, trying not to look as lost as he felt.

'You can go into Mr Culley's office now.'

Sandy glared at the pretentious twit in his purple suit, pink shirt, and dark pink tie. He so wanted to make a derogatory comment about the unnecessary rudeness, but didn't bother.

'Thanks for meeting me here,' Brad said, as he hugged his best friend.

'Ferdinand is rude to me. I don't enjoy coming here.'

Brad threw back his head. His laughter bounced off the walls in the sumptuous office. 'Don't take it so seriously. He likes to bait you. It works. Let's sit.'

The friends sat on armchairs that wrapped themselves around the person sitting in them. 'These are comfortable,' Sandy said, leaning back. 'I hadn't really noticed before. Where did you get them? I'll get some for my office.'

'No, you won't. They were $5000 each and imported from Italy.'

'Oh.' Sandy tried not to look disappointed. 'Why am I here?'

'Ebony is freaking out about seeing Sophie Marris in the café and nagging me to find out why she was there.'

'Nagging, eh? Seems just a few months ago, Ebony would be asking or encouraging. Now she's nagging. Trouble in paradise.'

'As I said the other day, at least I have a paradise. Let's move on. I've researched the place Ms Marris is supposed to be working at, another publishing company called Sleek Cat Books. Weird name. She could have met with a prospective author, though there aren't any authors from Altona on their website.'

'What do you want me to do?'

'Seriously, Sandy. Did I not just say you are to find out why she was in Altona?'

'No. You said Ebony was nagging *you* to find out what was going on. You are delegating that to me, are you?'

'Yes.' Brad handed Sandy a notebook with the date and time, location, and details of Ebony's sighting of Sophie Marris. 'My uncle is helping me with the mystery of Mum.'

Ferdinand pushed open the office door and put a tray on the coffee table.

'Thank you, Ferdinand,' Brad said, standing up to pass Sandy's latte to him.

'There's no sugar in his. I don't know if he takes it.'
Ferdinand gave Sandy the *you're not important to me* look as he left the room.

'Did you see the look he gave me?' Sandy whinged.

'Oh, forget it. Drink your coffee, eat the muffin, and get to work.'

Back in his own office with its cheaper than Brad's furniture, Sandy visited the Sleek Cat Books website looking for anything that would explain why Ms Marris was in Altona. The company appeared to be very different from Sapphire Publishing, not just in the books they published but their business model. This was a very stealthily disguised vanity publisher. The likelihood of Ms Marris chatting with a new author in a café in Altona, was very remote.

Sandy didn't trust Ms Marris, especially remembering she had an affair with Steven Culley. His initial hypothesis and one he would run with, was that Sophie Marris knew Ebony was in Altona – Steven did – and she was in the café to deliberately spook her. Was Sophie's companion Steven, or another bunny she had roped in?

Tomy had smuggled a copy of a case file format to Sandy on a memory stick the last time they caught up for dinner. He opened it and typed in the details of his first case as a private investigator for his own firm, *Nowhere to Hide Investigations*. He hadn't run the business name past Brad. He liked it, Tomy thought it was good, and he had already registered it.

Sandy scrolled through the contacts list on his phone, and pressed the button next to Sherryn Forbes's number. She answered after the second ring.

'Hi Sandy.'

'Hi, Ebony. Did Brad tell you he asked me to investigate Ms Marris and the café?'

'Yes. Any news?'

'She works for a vanity publisher so it's unlikely she was in that café meeting a prospective or current author. It appears that Sleek Cat Books is a quantity not quality outfit.'

'That surprises me. I hadn't met her, but she seemed devoted to her work. She was a very highly regarded editor. Why would she go down the publishing ladder like that?'

'I'll keep digging and let you know. When do you normally go to the café?'

'Monday and Thursday.'

'Don't go this Thursday. I'll go instead.'

Sophie Marris and Sandy had not met, but he wasn't prepared to take the risk that she would recognise him. A quick Google search would throw up his pic. He borrowed one of Brad's disguises and made his way to the café in Pier Street. While he waited to be shown to a table, he scanned the room. She was sitting with her back to him, in the far corner where Ebony saw her last week. She was alone.

When the waitress greeted Sandy and handed him a menu, he told her where he wanted to sit — on the opposite side of the café where he could see Ms Marris. He ordered a cappuccino and a pie and chips.

When she turned around to survey the room, Sophie's eyes skimmed right past him. Brad's blonde wig, beard, and moustache seemed to be working.

His lunch was uneventful. Sophie finished hers, looked around the room as she paid, and left. Sandy scoffed the last of his chips, gulped his coffee, hurried to the register, impatiently waved his phone over the eftpos machine stuck to the counter, and hurried out the door to follow Sophie Marris. He kept a good distance behind her so she couldn't see his reflection in shop front windows, but not too far that he would lose her. She crossed the street using the pedestrian crossing and walked to the car park behind the supermarket. He kept walking as she got into her new BMW SUV and left.

10

TOMY

Tomy's work mobile rang. She looked at the screen but didn't recognise the number. 'Hello. Detective Sergeant Tomy speaking.'

'Hello, Detective. Sophie Marris here.'

Silence.

'Detective?'

'Hello, Ms Marris. I'm sorry, you took me by surprise.'

'My neighbour gave me your card when I collected my cat from her. Is it alright to call you on this number?'

'If you are calling about police business, then yes.'

'It is. At least I think it is. Can we meet? I don't feel comfortable having important conversations over the phone.'

Tomy changed hands, putting her phone against the other ear. 'Are we going to have an important conversation? What about?'

'I'd rather not say on the phone. If you are not available, could Detective Sanderson help?'

'He resigned from the Force after your boyfriend made such a mess of so many people's lives.'

'He wasn't and isn't my boyfriend. Will you meet with me?'

'Yes. Where and when?'

———

Tomy toyed with calling Sandy, but decided against it. He was no longer a police member, and she didn't want to be in a position of wishing she could filter information. She would call him if the meeting with Ms Marris was useful.

She parked the car in a loading zone outside the Flinders Lane restaurant that Ms Marris had nominated, and put the *police* sign on the dashboard. Not being a native of Melbourne, she found the naming of the streets that ran on the northeast axis from south to north, weird at best. Flinders Street's little "brother" was Flinders Lane, where she was now. Little Collins Street was Collins Street's narrower self. Then Bourke Street and Little Bourke Street. Then Lonsdale and Little Lonsdale. The founding fathers seemed to have lost interest in the system after Little Lonsdale, because the next one was Latrobe Street. She made a mental note to learn more about the naming conventions of this city she had called home for several years.

The outside tables were full, so Tomy walked down the entrance corridor, past the rows of cakes and pastries that mocked her from behind their glass prison walls, and found a table in the middle of the café where she could see the door.

She put her hand on her hip in a reflex action when Sophie Marris startled her. 'You really shouldn't sneak up on an armed police officer.'

'I didn't sneak up. You were too busy staring at the

door. And you having a gun isn't the first thought that popped into my head.'

'Shh,' Tomy hissed, while moving her head from side to side to see if anyone had heard what Sophie said.

'I have a table over there. I've been here for thirty minutes. I've ordered coffee.' Sophie moved away toward the table she had chosen.

Tomy followed. 'I'm not late.'

'I know. I wanted to make sure no one followed me. Heaven knows how I was going to do that, though.' Sophie sipped her coffee. 'I am ordering lunch. The pizzas here are divine, as are the pasta dishes. Are you going to order?'

'Guess so. How do we do that?'

'Over at the counter. You can order a coffee there, too. And the water is on an island in the middle if you want to help yourself.'

'Come here often?' Tomy pushed back her chair.

'I used to. In my previous life.'

Sounds like Ebony Makepeace, Tomy said to herself while looking at the Italian favourites.

Her ordering complete, Tomy collected a jug of water and two glasses and headed back to the table. 'Why are you worried about being followed?' she asked, while getting settled and filling the glasses with water.

'I know Steven has absconded. We were an item for a little while. But he used me to get information about Ebony Makepeace.' She shook her head. 'How can someone with my education and life skills be so stupid? That was a rhetorical question.'

'Steven Culley manipulated lots of us, including

The Betrayal of Ebony Makepeace

his father and brother. I wouldn't lose any sleep over it.'

'Oh, but I do. A lot. I want to help you catch him.'

Tomy thanked the waitress as the pizza and coffee were put in front of her. When they were alone, she responded to Sophie's comment. 'How do you think you might do that?'

'I can contact him. No, before you ask, I will not tell you how. I can lure him out with the right bait.' Sophie took a mouthful of gnocchi and wiped her mouth with a serviette.

'If you know how to contact him and refuse to share that information, I can charge you with obstruction of justice. Just so you're aware.'

'But you won't, because then you will lose him forever.'

Tomy cut her pizza into smaller pieces and picked one piece up in her fingers. 'You don't eat pizza with a knife and fork,' she grumbled.

'I agree. Like toasted sandwiches. Ebony Makepeace, or Sherryn Forbes, uses a knife and fork to eat a cheese toasty.' Sophie sat back as if to assess Tomy's reaction.

Tomy looked at the woman opposite her, trying to work out if she could trust her. 'Is that so? How many times have you seen Ebony Makepeace eat a toasted sandwich?'

'Only twice. Both times at the café in Altona on Pier Street. The one she likes to frequent a couple of days a week. If I found her, so can others.'

'She saw you on one occasion.' Tomy picked up another piece of pizza.

'I thought she did.'

'She said you were with someone. A man.'

'My brother. I killed two birds with one stone — had lunch with my brother and spied on Ebony Makepeace at the same time.'

'Why are you spying on her?'

"Your questions are right to the point, aren't they, Detective Tomy?"

Tomy didn't answer. She picked up the last piece of the pizza and scoffed it down in a couple of bites.

'The reason I asked you to come today, Detective, is that I would like to meet with Ebony, or Sherryn, whatever she prefers to be called. Are you able to pass on my request?'

'I am. You realise she won't meet with you on her own.'

'I imagine she would bring Bradley. That's fine. I want to talk to her about her work, her writing. I'll wait to hear from you. Thanks for meeting me today.' Sophie Marris picked up her bag off the floor, pushed out her chair, reached out to shake Tomy's hand, and walked past the cake displays into Flinders Lane.

Before she started the car, Tomy called Sandy. 'Are you in your office?'

'Hello to you, too. You're getting more like Brad every day. Rude.'

'Are you? Simple question.'

'Yes.'

'I'll be there soon. Important stuff to talk about.' Tomy hung up, started the car, and drove the short distance from Flinders Lane to Docklands. She left the *police* sign on the dashboard and parked in a no-standing zone.

'This is good coffee,' Tomy said, making herself comfortable on the new couch Sandy had put in his office.

'Thank you. It's just one of those capsule machines, but you get lots of variety. The milk frother is excellent, heats the milk to a good temperature and froths it too.'

'I didn't ask for a product endorsement. Are you bored? Nothing to do?'

'Not really. I'm trying to help Brad. It's going to take a while to build up the business, I think. Just as well I don't have any financial pressures.'

'You'll get there,' Tomy said, putting her empty latte glass on a coaster on the coffee table. 'I had lunch with Sophie Marris.' Tomy watched Sandy's face change from nondescript to incredulous.

'Wow! What did she want?'

'She wants to meet with Ebony. I'm not going to get involved unless I think she is still associated with Steven Culley. I thought you might be interested.'

'Thanks, Tomy. I'll let Brad and Ebony know.'

11

BRAD

My uncle had emailed inviting me and "my lady friend" to visit for lunch on Saturday. Ferdinand, in his wisdom, didn't forward it to me until Friday afternoon. Odd. He's usually reliable and efficient.

After reading the email, I walked towards Ferdinand's desk.

'I know,' he said,, before I opened my mouth. 'I'm sorry. It came on Tuesday. I forgot.'

I didn't believe him, but there wasn't much I could do about it. If I had spidey senses, they would tingle about now.

'Don't give me that sulky face,' he said, packing up his desk for the early Friday afternoon escape.

'Have a nice weekend.' I walked back into my office and picked up my phone. Scrolling through my contacts to find my uncle's number, I pressed the call button.

'Hello, Brad.' He sounded miffed. Or was it my imagination? I would be miffed if I were him.

'My assistant forwarded your email about lunch tomorrow, exactly thirty minutes ago.'

'You need a new assistant. And you need a personal email address that he or she can't access.'

'You're right. Not something I'd thought about. He's always been so reliable.'

'Are you coming tomorrow?'

'If it's not too late.'

'No. It's fine. Will you be bringing anyone?'

'Yes, my partner, Sherryn Forbes.'

'Good, see you at midday.'

He hung up.

Uncle Walton was right. I needed a private email address. I started Google and set up a Gmail account. Only Uncle Walton, Ebony, and Sandy would have the address. I altered the email settings on my phone so that it would pick up the Gmail account.

I followed Ferdinand's lead and left the office early, navigating the tangle of traffic that starts building around three o'clock. That's the new peak hour, three o'clock until seven o'clock.

'You're home early.' Ebony pecked my cheek when I put my briefcase on the floor next to the couch. 'Don't leave it there. Put it in the study.'

Seriously! It had only been six months, and I felt as if I had been in this relationship for sixty years. 'I'll do it later. It's not going anywhere.'

Storm clouds washed over Ebony's face, but she said nothing. She probably thought glaring at the briefcase, then at me, then back at the briefcase would make me pick it up. It didn't.

'I had an email from my uncle on Tuesday, but Ferdinand didn't let me see until just before I left the office today.'

'That's not very efficient. In fact, it's rude.' Ebony

picked up my briefcase and put it at the foot of the stairs.

Oh for Pete's sake,' she won't let this go.

'Yes, it wasn't like him. Anyway, my uncle invited us to lunch tomorrow. He called you my "lady friend" in his email. Isn't that quaint?'

'Good grief, Brad. Where did quaint come from? The word is as old as your uncle calling me your lady friend.'

'I thought you'd like it.' I poured us both a glass of red, and I took mine to a reclining chair outside. Ebony followed. 'Are you ok to come tomorrow?' I asked, looking at her over the rim of the glass.

'I suppose so. More notice would have been good.'

I stopped myself from reaching over and choking her. Where had Ebony Makepeace gone? This really was Sherryn Forbes, and I didn't like her a lot of the time.

'He knows you as Sherryn Forbes,' I said, finishing my drink. 'Do you want to go out to get something to eat?'

She nodded, adding 'Well yes. It's your turn to cook and I see you didn't bring anything home.'

It's always my fucking turn to cook, the little gremlin in my head complained. I smiled, collected our glasses, and put them in the dishwasher. 'Where would you like to go?'

'The pub will do. It's Friday, there'll be a few people around. It's a friendly vibe.'

'The pub it is. I'll have a quick shower.'

'Take the briefcase upstairs on your way to the bathroom.' She couldn't help herself.

———

The Betrayal of Ebony Makepeace

Ebony sat stony faced, staring out the front window for half of the drive to Macedon. It was a long drive; not much to see but a pine tree plantation, a couple of properties dotted about here and there, and bush. As we passed the Woodend exit, I asked her what was wrong.

'I'd like us to have a chat when we get home from your uncle's. Life is not panning out the way I want it to.'

Ok then. Right back at you. 'Sure. Are you worried about Sophie Marris's appearance?'

'Yes. I guess I am. That's part of it. Let's not do this now while you are concentrating on the road.'

Oh yes. I am supposed to be concentrating on the road. But it's such a long and boring one.

'Tell me what to expect at your uncle's place.'

———

I pulled the car up in the driveway of my uncle's estate, expecting to press the button on the gate pillar to identify myself, but the gate opened without so much as a how do you do.

'Expecting us,' I said, glancing at Ebony. Her expression of awe as we crept up the expansive driveway sent waves of pride over me. I don't know why. It wasn't my house. *But it's been in the family for generations and might one day be mine.* My chest puffed out a little.

She scrambled out of the car before I turned off the ignition. 'It's magnificent, Brad. You didn't tell me.'

'Tell you what?'

'How wonderful it is. Do you think I could walk in the garden later? I can smell roses.'

This was a side of Ebony I hadn't seen. No idea she had a fondness for gardens. 'I'll mention it to Uncle Walton.'

She took my hand, and we made our way up the stairs to the front door.

Polo Shirt waved us in. 'Nice to see you again, Mr Culley,' he said, eyeing Ebony up and down.

'Thank you. This is my friend E...Sherryn Forbes.' *Oops, almost let that one slip.* 'I don't know your name. I'm sorry.'

'My name is Phillip. Very nice to meet you, Ms Forbes. This way.'

He led us through the house to the back verandah where Uncle Walton was perched on an egg chair. Ebony squeezed my hand. I didn't look at her. If she was grinning, I wouldn't be able to stop screeches of laughter.

'Bradley, my boy.' My uncle eased himself out of the chair and grabbed hold of it while he regained his balance. 'Phillip suggested we have lunch out here on the verandah. It is such a lovely day. He is joining us. Are you going to introduce me to your friend?'

'Oh, I am sorry, Uncle. This is my partner, Sherryn Forbes.'

Ebony stepped forward to match my uncle's body language and offered her hand. I looked around for the hand sanitizer. There it was, on the little table next to the egg chair.

'I'm very pleased to meet you, Ms Forbes.'

'And I you, Mr Warburton.' Ebony was the epitome of good manners.

'Please call me Walton. May I call you Sherryn?'

'Of course.' Ebony's smile was genuine. She seemed to be enjoying herself.

'Walton, at the risk of being presumptuous, would I be able to look around your beautiful garden after lunch?'

My uncle's face lit up like the fairy lights on a Christmas tree. 'Yes. I'll ask Phillip to accompany you. My knees are stuffed, I'm afraid. Especially the right one.'

I coughed into the crook of my arm. This man was surprising me more every minute.

'That sounds ominous, Bradley. Do you require a RAT?' [*Rapid antigen test.*]

'Thank you, Uncle, but no. The doctor said I have developed asthma. There's an inhaler in the car if I need it.' *This was a very sad sign of the times when sanitizer wiped away the warmth of the touch of another person's hand, and a cough sent people running for a COVID test.*

'Really? Your mother developed asthma in her thirties, too. Strange.'

I wanted to tell him I wasn't in my thirties, but let it slide.

He tilted his head indicating we should follow him around the corner. The verandah opened out onto an amazing deck that was bordered with an array of different sized pots, all the same colour, planted with rose bushes showing off at least six different colours.

Ebony gasped.

A table in the middle of the deck, under a cantilever umbrella, was set for lunch. Phillip brought a tray of drinks, put it on the table, and showed a woman who followed him, where to put the charcuterie board. I looked at Ebony. Her eyes were sparkling and the smile that spread over her face when we stepped on to the deck was fixed in place.

She obviously enjoyed seeing how the other half lived.

The four of us sat at the table, and Phillip passed around the food and drinks. Small talk accompanied our eating. I leant back in my chair and observed the vibe between Uncle Walton and Phillip. There didn't appear to be a relationship there, but Phillip was consumed with ensuring my uncle had everything he needed. Sipping his Champagne (yes I can call it that, because it was) my uncle seemed oblivious to Phillip's attentions. Phillip caught my eye, so I leant forward, cut off a small piece of Brie, and picked up a biscuit.

When we finished scoffing the food on the charcuterie board, Phillip cleared the table and went into the house. He returned twenty minutes later with another man, and a woman, who carried plates of sandwiches, and platters of salad.

'After lunch, Phillip will give you a tour of the gardens, Sherryn,' Uncle Walton said. 'And you and I will have a chat while they are wandering.' He looked at me and winked.

Who does that? Who winks at their adult nephew? I don't even remember him doing that when I was a child. The man reveals stranger things about himself with each visit.

We polished off the sandwiches a little more slowly than the cheese and nibbles. They were delicious, and Ebony gushed to Phillip and Walton about how lovely everything was, and how thoughtful of them to include vegetarian options.

As if on cue, Phillip pushed back his chair and asked Ebony to join him in the garden. She almost skipped down the stairs and onto a path.

'Let's go into my office,' my uncle said, pushing himself up with the support of the table.

'Are you alright?' He struggled to take a step.

'Been sitting down too long. The knees lock up. Especially the right one. I'll be ok when I move.'

I stood back and waited while my uncle's legs obeyed his brain and he walked into the house.

'Don't you think you should do something about that?' I asked, as he showed me where to sit in his office.

'You sound like Phillip. Yes. I'll go to the GP and get a referral to my orthopaedic surgeon. The last time I went he told me to hang on for a bit — yes, his words. They like you to wait as long as possible, because the replacements only last fifteen or twenty years.'

'Seems barbaric to me. Considering the obvious pain you are in.' I wanted to add that the pain aged him and that he looked a lot older than the early sixties he admitted to.

'You sit down. I'll stand for a while.'

I sat in a club chair that was surprisingly comfortable. While my uncle walked around the room, he told me to look through the papers on the coffee table.

On top of the pile was the probate for my mother's estate and a copy of her Will. I looked up at him. He nodded, saying I should read the document.

My mother had written her Will when she and Father bought into the mining business some twenty-five years ago. She'd left everything to Father. The Will said the Minors *(this is how the name of the trust is spelt)* Trust she set up for my brother and I when we were children, would be managed by her executor if she died before we each reached thirty years. The maturity age of the Trust.

'Was Steven aware of the Trust?' I asked my uncle, as he made his fourth lap of the room.

'I don't know. Possibly. Either Mina or your father could have told him. I didn't. Over the years, the Trust has grown to a substantial amount. Did you look at the figures?'

'No. I think it's grubby.'

'You and Steven have three million dollars each. I'll be managing the Trust as your mother's executor.'

I felt my uncle's eyes boring into the back of my head. He had stopped pacing and stood behind my chair.

'I don't care how much it is, Uncle Walton. Right now, I only care about whether my brother knows about it.'

The pain in my uncle's knees must have subsided with the movement because he sat opposite me.

'There is something else to discuss with you, Bradley.' He shuffled the papers on the table and brought a purple folder to the top of the pile. 'My Will.'

'Please, Uncle. I don't want to be involved. We haven't been close in the last few years. What you do with your estate is up to you.'

'You are correct. But I am leaving you and Steven this house with funds to maintain it. From the grave, I won't be able to stop either of you from selling it, but I would like it to stay in the family. Phillip is getting twenty-five percent of the rest. You and Steven twenty-five percent to share equally. Twenty-five percent to my favourite charity, and the remaining twenty-five percent is to be distributed amongst the staff who have been with me for five years or more.'

My uncle sat back in his chair and clasped his hands across his middle.

'Thanks for letting me know,' I said, 'but it will be some time before we need to think about that. Hopefully Steven dies before you. If he does, I'll give his share to Phillip.'

He smiled, nodding in agreement.

'You and Phillip are not a couple, are you, Uncle?'

I'd never heard him laugh as loudly. It was contagious. A smile spread across my face.

'Oh, Bradley. You are funny. No. I sometimes wonder if Phillip would like us to be. But we sit on opposite sides of that fence. I have had lady friends over the years, but never anyone who had me smitten like Wilhelmina did to Douglas. Phillip has his own friends. He lives in the cottage on the other side of the tennis court. I don't keep track of his relationships. He and Sherryn should be back from the tour soon. Let's return to the verandah.'

'Your uncle is delightful, Brad. And Phillip is the sweetest man. He gave me cuttings from the roses and said I was welcome to go there any time.'

We were driving down the Calder Freeway, and Ebony hadn't stopped gushing about Walton and Phillip. I was pleased she had an enjoyable afternoon, but switched off when the chatter moved to the names of the various rosebushes and other plants growing through the estate.

'Brad. Brad! You're not listening to me, are you?'

'No. Not really. My attention is wandering, trying to keep my mind on the road.'

'What did your uncle want to see you about while Phillip and I were in the garden?'

I didn't want Ebony to know about Uncle Walton's Will. Talking about what would happen when he dies, seemed like tempting fate to me. I left that part out.

'He showed me the probate for Mum's Will. We talked about what to do with Steven's share.'

'Oh. Is there anything you can do?'

'Not really. It will have to stay in trust until he's found either dead or alive. If he's not found within seven years, it will go to me. If he is located and found guilty of serious crimes, it will stay where it is until they release him. If he dies in jail, the executor of his estate will deal with it.

Ebony fidgeted in her seat and stared out the passenger side window for a few moments. 'Is it a lot of money?'

'Yes. But it's still tied up because Father is dead, and she left everything to him. I don't envy my uncle having to manoeuvre his way through it all.' I didn't tell her about the Minors Trust.

Whether it was good manners or reluctance to press me, Ebony didn't ask any more questions about mine and my uncle's chat. She did, however, remind me she wanted us to talk when we got home. *Great*. She turned on the radio and connected her phone via Bluetooth, telling Google to play her favourite music. Didn't seem to matter that it was my car, and I don't like much of the stuff she listens to. The last half of the journey was long.

12

EBONY

'Thanks for taking me today.' Ebony took off her shoes and put them at the foot of the stairs to take up with her the next time she went to the bedroom.

Brad put his shoes next to hers, put the car keys on the hooks she'd organised near the garage door, and slumped on the couch. 'It was a nice afternoon. I've never spent that much time with my uncle, let alone eating with him when it wasn't a big family affair.'

'Going up there today reiterated my qualms about staying here.' Ebony sat in the chair opposite the couch. 'We need to talk.'

'I'm listening.' Brad sat up straight, crossed his legs, and looked at the woman who had changed his life so dramatically.

'I have strong feelings for you, Brad, but I don't love you anymore. And although I enjoy the writing group and like the café, it's time I got my own place. Being a kept woman doesn't sit well with me.' Ebony waited for Brad's face to show a flicker of emotion, of surprise, of anything. It was blank.

'This is a shock. I knew things weren't the same between us, but until now I wasn't really worried.'

'You've been short with me. Rude sometimes. It's as if I'm an afterthought and a nuisance. Flitting off to your uncle's in the late afternoon without thinking about me having been alone all day is an example of how you make me feel. When it's your turn to organise dinner, it's always a drama. The only time you're interested in my day is when I say something shocking, like I saw Sophie Marris at the café.' Ebony got a tissue out of her pocket and wiped under her eyes.'

'Oh, Eb. Don't cry.'

'I'm not crying. I'm emotional. It's taken a long time to work up the courage to have this talk.'

Brad squirmed a little on the couch. He crossed and uncrossed his legs a few times. Eventually, he got up and knelt in front of her.

'I'm sorry. I've been a bastard. Taking you for granted, being short with you, not caring about your feelings, let alone how you are coping. It's only been a matter of months since we met.'

Ebony laughed sarcastically. 'You could call it a meeting, I suppose.'

Brad stood up and moved back to the couch. 'What would you like me to do? What would you like to happen?'

Ebony folded her arms. 'We will start by spending some time apart. I will find a place of my own.'

'That seems a tad silly when we have two. You stay here and I'll go back to South Melbourne.'

Ebony knew it wasn't a sacrifice for Brad to move; he hadn't wanted to live in Altona in the first place. He hated the seaweed smell as it wafted from the bay when the tide went out and the wind blew from the south. He hated how the area swelled with people in the warmer months, and he hated that his property was on Boulevard, not *The* Boulevard. When he told someone the address, he complained about the road's name.

'Gee, you will really put yourself out for me?' Ebony didn't hide the venom in her voice.

'I love you, Ebony. I loved you the first moment I saw you walking into the café in North Melbourne. Your hair looking as if it hadn't been washed for weeks, the op-shop clothes you wore with pride, and the clunky boots which clomped loudly on the footpath. I knew it was all an act, that there was a strong, stylish woman under the disguise. But when I sat opposite you in the café the day I shot you, I had doubts — that day you looked particularly drab.'

'Don't hold back.'

'I think the dramas we have been through together made us stronger people. Don't you?'

'Dramas? Losing the life I knew, watching my parents and friends grieve for me, believing me to be dead, uprooting my life and inventing another one, is more than a "drama". Ebony used air quotes to emphasise the word.

'I'll move out tomorrow if you like. Give you some time to yourself.' He glanced at his pocket as the vibration of his phone took his attention.

'Best answer that,' Ebony snarled.

'If it's important, they will leave a message. We need to work on us. Would you like a coffee and something to eat?'

'A coffee would be good, thank you. I am still full from lunch, so I don't want anything to eat just yet.'

Brad moved over to Ebony and kissed her forehead. 'I do love you.'

While he put fresh coffee beans and water into the

coffee machine, his phone vibrated again. He let it go. Then Ebony's rang.

'It's Sandy.'

Brad took his phone out of his pocket. 'It was him calling me. Best see what he wants.'

———

Sandy pecked Ebony on the cheek when she opened the door to let him in. 'Hi. Are we in the family room?'

'I guess so.' Ebony closed the door and followed him.

'Coffee?' Brad asked when Sandy appeared.

'Sure. And a biscuit. One of those Italian ones. Thanks.'

'Biscotti,' Ebony said to Brad when she noticed the frown.

Sandy sat where Brad had been sitting and asked Ebony how she was.

'Don't bother with small talk while you wait for your coffee, Sandy.'

'Ok, then. As I said on the phone, I have something important to share, so I'll wait till Brad sits down. That way, I won't have to repeat myself.'

It annoyed Ebony that she had to wait for Brad. This was another thorn in her side. She wasn't as important. But she didn't say anything to Sandy.

Brad put a tray on the coffee table, picked up one of the cups and sat at the other end of the couch. 'Yours is there,' he said to Sandy. 'Are the biscuits up to scratch?'

'Thanks for going to all this trouble,' Sandy muttered. 'Is there sugar in mine?'

Brad ignored him and asked what was happening.

The Betrayal of Ebony Makepeace

'Sophie Marris contacted Tomy. They met in the city. Ms Marris said she wants to meet with you, Ebony.'

Ebony put down her coffee cup. 'Why?'

'Something about your writing. Tomy doesn't know whether to trust her, and suggested that you don't meet her alone.'

'If I go, will you come with me?' she asked Sandy.

Sandy looked sideways at Brad. His face was blank. 'You and Brad should go. I'll watch from a distance just in case Steven shows up.'

Ebony saw Brad's expression change from calm to agitated, to tense. 'Brad, what do you think?'

'I'm suss. I don't trust her. She was sleeping with Steven. It might be a trap. We will consider your safety before we agree to a meeting.'

Ebony noticed the careful way Brad spoke. Before she'd said she wanted a break, he would have decided without even contemplating her position. 'I don't trust her, either. Surely she could speak to me over the phone?'

'That's a good point, Ebony,' Sandy said. 'But she might have more to say. She knows your new name, knows you live in Altona, knows which café you frequent. She could be dangerous. Might be worth placating her with a face-to-face meeting.'

'How did she find out? When is all of this going to end?' Ebony picked up the empty coffee cups and thumped them down on the kitchen bench. 'I'm going upstairs. I need to focus. Thanks Sandy.'

13

BRAD

I was happy enough to move out of the Altona house, but not to leave Ebony. In my little mind, I had envisaged us moving into my place in South Melbourne once she'd got her life settled. Getting her life settled now seemed almost unachievable; Sophie Marris had seen to that. In the four days since Sandy dropped the Sophie Marris bombshell, Ebony hadn't left the house. She said she was working out her options. I kept away, waiting for those options to see the light of day.

Ferdinand didn't look up from his keyboard when I walked into the office. 'Good morning, boss,' I trumpeted.

He jumped. 'You startled me. Don't do that again,' he complained.

'How will I know not to startle you again? What's going on? I walked in like I usually do.'

'Go and sit at your desk, get organised for the day. I'll be along in a few minutes. I have information to share with you.'

It never ceased to amaze me how I was the employer and Ferdinand the employee, yet he was the one who usually called the shots. I obeyed him.

While I was waiting for my computer to decide to jump into the land of the living, Ferdinand came in and sat down in the chair on the other side of my desk. He thumped a bundle of files on the nice clean surface. I frowned.

Without even looking up he said, 'Don't roll your eyes, or frown, or whatever it is you just did. We have work to do.'

'Why do we have paper to wade through? Aren't all our clients' records on computer?'

Ferdinand sighed the sigh of exasperation and frustration. 'This is Sapphire Publishing's stuff. You told me to go through it. The early records were not transferred to digital.'

'Oh.'

'Does that humble pie taste good?' Ferdinand leant back in the chair and folded his arms across his chest, glaring at me.

'I apologise, Ferdinand. I am grateful for your diligence.'

His ego massaged sufficiently for us to proceed, he opened the file that sat on top and turned it around for me to see. 'This is the most interesting thing I found.' He pointed toward the middle of the page.

Sapphire Publishing, a business that was just there, whose significance in my father's life I had no understanding of, or sadly no care for, suffered when my father died. The statement Ferdinand pointed at showed a bank balance of five hundred dollars.

I looked up at Ferdinand. 'Any idea what's happened?'

'Sort of. Look at the statements. The money disappeared in small increments fortnightly, until your father died, then in larger amounts at shorter intervals until it was all gone. My theory is that whoever took it knew you, or another accountant, prepared the Business Activity Statement for the tax office each quarter, and took small amounts before a BAS report was due, then the rest before the next one. That's how I found all this, getting ready to do the BAS.'

'Fuck.' There was no other word in my vocabulary that fitted the situation. 'How are we just finding this now?'

My uncle didn't answer my call. I left a message asking him to contact me as soon as possible. I waited until the end of the day, then called him again.

'Mr Warburton is indisposed,' Phillip grumbled into my ear.

'That's lovely for him, Phillip, whatever you mean. It is important he call me back. How long will his indisposal last?'

I know that isn't a word, but Phillip's games were tiresome and there wasn't much I could do to annoy him.

'He is with a client. I'll let him know. Goodbye, Mr Culley.'

'Pretentious, much?' I snarled, putting my mobile on my desk.

Ferdinand and I spent the best part of the day working through Sapphire Publishing's accounts, putting together a report detailing the exodus of the money. Over a coffee and a dinner box from Macca's [*this is the colloquial name Australians use for McDonald's*] we finished up. I was still waiting for my uncle to call me back.

'Not in a hurry to toddle off to see Miss Forbes?'

The tilt of Ferdinand's head and the smirk on his face made me want to slap him. 'I've moved back into my South Melbourne place. She wants to be alone for a while.' His question and the stress of the day had taken the wind out of my sails. I wasn't up to the sarcastic banter.

'Oh, I'm sorry.'

He sounded genuine, but didn't look it.

'Let's call it a day.' I picked up the files in front of me, reached over for the ones in front of Ferdinand, and turned off the computer.

'Aren't you going to wait here until your uncle calls you?' Ferdinand pushed in his chair and followed me out of my office.

'No. My guess is Phillip will closet him away. He probably doesn't even know I called. If I don't hear from him, you and I will pay him a visit.'

Ferdinand got out of the elevator on the ground floor. He lived at Docklands in one of those apartment blocks that are half empty, but he had an amazing view over the expanse of Port Phillip Bay. No struggling through traffic for him. I didn't even know if he had a driver's licence. He reminds me of the Will and Grace characters on the television show. They never left New York. Ferdinand never leaves Melbourne.

'See you in the morning.' He waved as the doors closed on his what seemed to be forced smile.

I made my way down to the parking garage under the building and put the files on the back seat of my car. As I pulled into the traffic, the dash display lit up with my uncle's name. I pushed answer.

'Hello, Uncle Walton.'

'It's Phillip. Your uncle has gone to bed early. He will call you in the morning.'

I didn't respond. Didn't complain. I pushed the button to disconnect the call. Is this normal? Is this how the ultra-rich live? Having someone else be your mouthpiece? My uncle didn't seem the sort of person who would let another run his life. But what did I know?

A wave of despair washed over me when I opened the garage door and drove in. The last time I was in my South Melbourne townhouse alone, my brother kidnapped me. Since then, Ebony had come with me whenever I wanted to pick up something, check the mail, open a window. The despair morphed into anxiety when I stood in the hallway all by myself. Making my way to the kitchen, I turned on every light switch I passed. By the time I'd put the files on the dining table, turned on the television, put on the kettle, and changed out of my suit and tie, the whole downstairs was lit up like Luna Park. It didn't make me feel any better, though.

Using the milk frother attached to my coffee machine, I made a hot chocolate and sat at the dining table, files spread out in front of me. I double checked the figures, the dates, the signatures. The more I looked, the more convinced I was that Steven had embezzled from Sapphire Publishing.

The Betrayal of Ebony Makepeace

My phone danced around on the table as it vibrated to let me know someone was calling. Ebony.

'Hi, my love,' I said with genuine affection.

'I met with Sophie Marris today.'

14

EBONY

Through the screen in the kitchen, linked to the security cameras outside the house, Ebony saw Brad's SUV pull out of the garage. She monitored the display while he sat in the driveway for a few minutes. When he had finally driven away, Ebony got out the prepaid phone she'd bought at the supermarket and turned it on. Reading the number written on the back of Tomy's business card, she dialled.

The call was answered on the second ring. 'Hello?'

'Sophie? Ebony asked.

'Yes. Hello. Good to hear from you. Please tell me what you want me to call you.'

'Sherryn will be fine,' Ebony said. Wondering why she'd used that name when Sophie Marris knew her story.

'Ok. Sherryn. We need to chat, to talk. Meet me at Southern Cross Station, at the Collins Street end, Thursday morning at eleven.'

Ebony's breath left her lungs in a gush. She'd been holding it in for a minute or more. 'Why that location? And why do we need to see each other?'

'It's busy. We will melt into the crowd. We will

catch another train, so come prepared to be away for the day. See you then.'

Ebony stared at the phone while its display dissolved into black. She decided not to tell Brad, and instead, tidied up the kitchen, put her laptop under her arm, made her way upstairs, and checked the train timetables for Thursday.

―――

Ebony tapped her Myki card and made her way to the Collins Street end of Southern Cross Station. Although she and Sophie had never met in person, her picture was on Sapphire Publishing's website.

'Follow me,' a woman in jeans and a bright red jacket said as she pushed passed Ebony.

Sophie Marris led Ebony to the regional train platforms, waved her Myki card through the gate and kept walking. Ebony followed suit. Sophie boarded the Ballarat train. Ebony walked further down the platform and stepped into another carriage. The carriages had walk-throughs — she could move later.

'Where are we going, and why?' Ebony asked, when Sophie sat opposite her.

'We will get off at Bacchus Marsh and find a little spot to chat and have something to eat.'

'Why the subterfuge?' Ebony fished her Myki out of her pocket and handed it to the conductor to check.

'I am not sure if I'm being followed.' Sophie looked over her shoulder and down the aisle into the next carriage.

'Well that puts us up shit creek if you are.'

'No one has followed us on to the train, at least.' Sophie showed the conductor her Myki card.

'I don't understand why anyone would follow you. I am the one they wanted to kill.' Ebony stared out the window as the train sped through the North Melbourne station.

'Doesn't it stop at the stations?' she asked Sophie.

'Have you never been on a regional train?'

'No. I live in Altona. It's hardly regional. And before that I was in North Melbourne. That couldn't be more removed from regional. But you know where I live.' Ebony scowled at the woman sitting opposite.

'Regional trains stop at a few stations in the suburban network for country travellers to get on. Going into the city, they stop for country travellers to get off. It's a very civilised way to travel.'

'Lovely. Now tell me why we are doing this.' Ebony folded her arms across her chest.

'Did you know I was sleeping with Steven Culley when he was manipulating my employer, his father, and overseeing yours and Brad's demise?'

Ebony nodded. 'Not at the time it was going on, but later.'

'Naturally, when I found out what was happening, I stopped seeing him. A non-event really, because he was arrested and then disappeared.'

'Do you know where he is?' Ebony glared at Sophie, ready to react to a lie.

'No. I haven't had contact with him since he kidnapped Brad. How is Brad, by the way?'

Ebony ignored the question. 'Why are we doing this?'

Sophie took off her jacket and crossed her legs. 'If I found you, Steven can too. I don't think you are safe.'

'You need to catch up, Sophie. Steven knows where

The Betrayal of Ebony Makepeace

I am. He spat it in Brad's face before he was about to have him killed.'

'Then why are you still there?' Sophie's voice bounced off the train carriage walls. 'You know what he is capable of. This is our stop. We'll finish this over coffee and food.'

Ebony followed Sophie off the train and walked with her towards the main street of Bacchus Marsh. Ebony was impressed with the preserved old buildings and the wide streets, but neither woman spoke until Sophie pointed out a café she said would be suitable.

Ebony chose a poached egg and avocado on toast, adding a soy latte just before the waitress turned her attention to Sophie. Sophie ordered a salad and a pot of green tea.

'Are you writing again?' Sophie asked, when the waitress left, and they were alone.

'A bit. Let's get back on track. Back to Steven.'

'I think he is still in Melbourne.' Sophie looked at Ebony with pity in her eyes. 'He hasn't contacted me, but he has too much going on here to just walk away. There will be minions doing his bidding, shuffling around money and assets, and avoiding scrutiny. When he's tied up all the things he wants to, I worry that you and Brad will be on his list again.'

This new information swirled around in Ebony's brain like snowflakes, and when her lunch arrived, she discovered she had lost her appetite. She played with the egg for a while, then pushed her plate away.

'Not hungry?' Sophie quizzed.

'Not after a bombshell like that, I'm not. I was feeling as if I might have a chance at a normal life. That's hilarious, isn't it?'

'I'm sorry. He is dangerous.'

'Oh, der.' Ebony asked the waitress where the bathroom was, and made her way to it.

'I've paid,' Sophie said, when Ebony returned to her seat.

'You didn't have to do that. But thank you. Are we going?'

'Yes. What you do with the information is up to you, Sherryn. If you are writing again, submit your manuscript to my new employer. Here's my card.'

Ebony put it in her pocket.

When the train stopped at Footscray on the way back to Melbourne, Ebony said goodbye to Sophie and got off. She caught a suburban train to Altona, thinking how she much preferred the regional rail. *Perhaps I'll move to the country.*

15

BRAD

I moved the phone away from my ear and looked at it. Why? Was I trying to make sure I was talking to Ebony? I waited for more from her. I couldn't think of anything to say.

'Brad?'

'Yes. I'm here. Sorry. I thought you said you met with Sophie Marris today.'

'Don't be cute. I'm not in the mood. It's been stressful. Can you organise a time for you and Sandy to come here? We have a lot to unpack.'

I absolutely hate the word "unpack" in this context. Unpacking is what you do when you get back from holidays, or when you've moved house. It's one of the trendy jargon words that irk me.

'Sure,' I said, as cheerfully as possible. 'Are you ok?'

'Not really. There is a lot to process. Let me know when you can come over.'

She hung up. Rude.

I pondered over Ebony meeting with Sophie for a few minutes before I called Sandy. I was hurt that she hadn't told me about the meeting, that she hadn't included me, that she was pulling away from me more quickly than I cared to think about. Whatever.

'When are you available to come with me to see Ebony?'

'Geez Louise, you are getting worse and worse by the day. You couldn't be any ruder if you tried,' Sandy snarled into the phone.

'Yes, I could, actually.'

'I bet. Why do I have to go with you?'

'She met with Sophie Marris today, apparently. Just told me about it, and wants you and me to go to her place when we can.' I realised I'd told Sandy Ebony and I weren't together without even mentioning it.

'You've moved out of the place in Altona, then?' Sandy asked, a smirk hidden away in the question.

'For the time being. She wants time out and I have a lot going on with my family at the moment. Least of all with Steven.'

'Seems as if we have some catching up to do, too, Brad. Do you want to meet me at Claude's?

'I can't tonight, Sandy. I've got lots of paperwork to go through. I'll come to your office tomorrow. Midmorning. Does that suit?

'Sadly, yes,' Sandy groaned. 'I'm not exactly overwhelmed with work.'

I wasn't prepared to deal with Sandy's new business woes, so I said I'd see him tomorrow and hung up.

It was hard to concentrate on the work I'd brought home, so I put a frozen dinner in the microwave and turned on the TV while I waited seven minutes to hear the beep of "finished". All the scenarios set themselves out on a chessboard in my mind, and moved to places they thought were relevant or appropriate. I studied them while I ate the processed food and half listened to the television.

I sent Ferdinand a text to say I was meeting Sandy first thing and would be in as soon as possible. He responded with a grumpy face emoji.

Sandy's new office bore the semblance of a professional workspace. He had filled it with good quality furniture, which was well placed and looked welcoming. 'You've been busy, I see.'

'No thanks to you. I seem to remember you were going to help me.' He held up his hand to stop me from responding. 'Tomy helped. She has a good eye, don't you think?' Sandy scanned the room approvingly before sitting on the couch opposite me.

'Do you need two couches, though? Seems pretentious.'

'You are an arsehole, you know.'

There was a shard of guilt stuck in my throat. 'I'm sorry, Sandy. I have been ignoring you. The office looks great. Tomy has done well. I have a job for you.'

The scowl slid down his face and he replaced it with an expression of interest. 'Go on.'

I filled Sandy in on Sapphire Publishing and Steven's subterfuge.

'And you are certain all the money has gone, not just transferred to another account or another business?' Sandy handed me a coffee that he had made in his new capsule machine.

'Thank you.' I wanted to scream at him that I only drank coffee from a real coffee machine, but Ebony had a capsule one and I accepted it without drama. Best to keep quiet. 'Yes we are certain. I went through all the records last night. The money is missing. I'm waiting to hear from my uncle. To get his opinion. I'll have to go and see him.'

'Do you want me to come with you?'

I looked off into the distance to mull over Sandy's offer. But decided against accepting. 'Not this time. Ferdinand and I will go as soon as we can. For now we need to focus on Sophie Marris.'

'What did she say to Ebony?'

'Ebony didn't elaborate. She was quite short with me to be honest.'

I noticed Sandy trying to stop a grin from spreading across his face. 'Is that funny, is it?' Couldn't help myself.

'Yes it is. You are short with me all the time. How does it feel?'

'Point taken. When are you available to come with me to Altona?'

'Whenever you are.'

———

I sent Ebony a text saying Sandy and I would be there around six that evening. I could see her rolling her eyes as she read the message. I'm psychic. Sandy would say I'm psycho too. Whatever. I knew six wasn't convenient for her. She liked to prepare dinner then. I'll order in if it's appropriate.

Sandy parked his car next to mine in the car park, got out, and pressed the button to lock it. Before I said anything, he was in the passenger seat of my SUV, and clipping in his seat belt. 'You don't have to worry about me speeding, dear,' I said, while checking the flow of vehicles. 'We have to go on the stupidly named freeway, so we'll be sitting in traffic for ages.'

'It's getting worse, isn't it?' Sandy asked, while fiddling with his phone. 'I think it's all the infrastructure work that's going on.'

Good Lord. A genius. 'Hmm.' I nodded.

I parked in the street outside the Altona townhouse, making it clear by that action that I wasn't taking Ebony for granted.

'Wow, she has sent you to Coventry,' Sandy snickered. 'Not allowed to use the garage.'

I ignored him and locked the car as soon as he shut the passenger door.

Ebony didn't wait for us to knock. Thanks to me installing it, the camera system would have alerted her to our arrival. She opened the door and hugged Sandy. I left it to her how she was going to greet me. She pecked me on the cheek.

Ebony waved her hand to point at the furniture in the family room. 'Take a seat. I haven't started dinner. It's too early. I thought we could worry about that later.'

Before the disappointment settled in my gut, I noticed the antipasto platter and the wineglasses on the coffee table. 'This looks very nice. Thank you,' I said politely.

Ebony poured us all a glass of wine before sitting in the armchair between the two couches. 'I have a lot to tell you both.'

When the events of her meeting with Sophie Marris were laid out before us, Sandy gave me a look indicating he wasn't happy. I asked him what he was thinking.

'I don't trust her. I'm worried for your safety, Ebony, and think you should move from here. There's no advantage in Steven killing you now, but that doesn't mean he won't find a way to use you to get to someone else.'

'What do you mean, get to someone else?' Ebony's voice got higher at the end of the question.

'By the information Brad has shared with me recently, I think he will do anything to get his hands on the Culley family wealth. Such as it is. I wouldn't put it past him to use you as a means to an end.'

I watched the colour drain from her face. It seemed to slide down her neck and disappear into her clothing.

'But she told me she isn't seeing Steven. So why does my meeting with her cause you such concern?' Ebony waited for Sandy's response.

'I told you. I don't trust her. Just because she says she isn't seeing Steven doesn't mean that's true. How do we know he isn't working her behind the scenes?'

I stood up. 'Sandy and I will stay here tonight. In the morning, you'll pack some things. You need to relocate.'

I gave the keys to my black SUV to Sandy and closed the garage door after he drove out. Ebony was upstairs packing a few things. I could hear her sobbing. She had wanted to leave on her own terms, not being forced to run away and hide again. We reached a compromise last night: she would leave with Tomy this morning, but relocate to a place of her choosing until once again things had settled down.

Tomy sent me a text when she was in the lane at the back of the townhouse.

'Tomy is here,' I said to Ebony from the bedroom door. 'Are you all set?'

'Do I look all set?' Her eyes were red and swollen from crying.

My heart ached for her. I wanted to put my arms around her and shield her from all the drama, but when I tried that last night, she shoved me away. To be pragmatic, I decided not to buy into her grief.

'I'll carry your bags. The light in the family room is on. Don't turn it off. Turning off lights is something people do when they are leaving the house or going to bed. If anyone is watching, they will have seen Sandy drive away in my car.'

'I imagine you are saying this from your extensive stalking experience.' The hiss was evident in her tone. I didn't respond.

Tomy waited in the courtyard. Ebony opened the sliding door and stepped outside. Taking the bags, Tomy nodded to me and walked toward the gate at the back of the garden that led to the rear laneway. She waited for Ebony.

'Let me know when you arrive at your destination,' I said, holding back the unfamiliar urge to cry.

'I'm not going to do that.' Ebony folded her arms and gave me a look. The same look she gave me the first time we met in the café in North Melbourne. 'It's better if you don't know where I am.' She turned and walked towards Tomy.

'I love you, Eb.' My words hung around the back gate like a bad smell.

16

EBONY

Ebony got into the passenger seat of Tomy's car, did up her seat belt, and looked across at the detective sergeant. 'Do you think anyone will follow us?'

'Doesn't matter. We'll go to my office first and when you are ready to leave, you'll go in a different car. The Police Department car park is secured, so we can't be followed into it.'

'Thanks for all you are doing for me, Tomy.'

'No worries. Might even lead us to Steven Culley. You never know.'

True to her word, as soon as Ebony had finished a coffee and pastry, Tomy arranged for another car and another police member to drive her – wherever.

'Take up the brace position,' the plain-clothed police officer said to Ebony as he lumbered into the driver's seat. 'Like on a plane. Flatten yourself so you are hard to see. Where am I driving to?'

'Footscray railway station.'

Getting out of the car, Ebony thanked the officer for his help.

'All good. You take care. I'll pop the boot.'

He stayed in the car while Ebony lifted out her bags and settled them on the asphalt of the drop-off area. She closed the boot and made her way to the platforms. She took her phone out of her pocket to check the time — 12.10pm. From her research before she went to bed last night, the next train to Wendouree was due at Footscray at 12.44pm on platform four. Ebony wheeled her bags to the group of shops near the station and bought a coffee and a spring roll.

She tapped her Myki on the turnstile reader, and once on the platform, put her coffee cup on top of the largest bag and pushed the spring roll up from its hiding place in the little paper cocoon. She hadn't had one of these since before she was "killed". While she stood savouring the long-lost joy of the crisp pastry and hot vegetable filling rolling around in her mouth, Ebony's eyes darted over the other platforms. She felt stupid. If anyone was following her, she wouldn't know. No one knew where she was going. Not even Brad, who kept his word and wasn't bothering her.

Surprised so many people were on the train in the middle of the day, Ebony made her way up the aisle to find a seat that faced the way she was travelling. She put her large bag on the overhead shelf and climbed over a man's legs to get to the seat, resting the smaller bag on her lap. Checking her emails on her phone, she let out a breath she didn't realise she was holding when she saw the email from Airbnb. It showed the code to unlock the mailbox for the key to the cottage she was renting long term. She put the code in a document on her phone and scanned the rest of her inbox. An email from Brad asking her to take care of herself, and to let him know when she was ready to talk, made its way to the recycle bin. At least he wasn't bombarding her with texts; she would hate to find it necessary to block his number.

Larger properties surrounded the cottage, but it was on the edge of Lake Wendouree, offering beautiful views from the living room and front verandah. The furniture was contemporary and comfortable, the cottage clean and fresh. The hosts had been considerate and put a litre of milk, half a dozen eggs, and a small tub of butter in the fridge. A loaf of sourdough bread, tucked up in a brown paper bag, sat on the bench next to little sachets of Vegemite and jam. Tea, coffee, and sugar were on the other side next to the toaster and electric kettle. Ebony let a feeling of calm wash over her as she unpacked her bags.

Deciding to save the food for a light dinner, Ebony put on her sneakers and a jacket, put her small handbag over her shoulder so that it sat in front, and pulled the cottage door closed. She'd stayed in Wendouree when she was Ebony Makepeace. Stayed with her best friend Gabrielle in a house not unlike this one. They'd walked the six kilometres around the lake on three of the five days they'd stayed. *Not today, though.*

Ebony stood on the track that wound its way around the perimeter of the lake and called up Google Maps on her phone. It picked her location instantly, and showed it was a forty-eight-minute walk to the main Wendouree shopping centre. She opened the taxi app and ordered a ride: food shopping and a new pillow were on her list.

17

BRAD

'Assume you are being watched.' Sandy handed me the keys to my SUV and sat down in the chair on the other side of my desk.

'It won't matter if I'm being watched, will it? Sophie Marris said Ebony was the one in danger.'

'After what your brother did to you, I would be a bit on edge if I were you.'

I decided not to encourage Sandy in his assumptions, so led him off track. 'Can you take a close look at the autopsy report on my mother's body? My uncle emailed it. He said she died of a brain aneurism.'

I printed the email and passed it over the desk. Sandy leant back, crossed his legs, and frowned as he read the report. 'Nothing appears to be amiss. What's the next step?' he asked, putting the report back on my desk.

'I don't know. You're the friggin' detective.' My snarl was over the top, and I immediately regretted it. 'Sorry. I'll call Ferdinand in, and we can go over what we have. You might come up with something we haven't thought of.'

Sandy nodded, he knew me well, and accepted my apology as if it were handed to him on a silver platter.

Ferdinand brought in his share of the paperwork, and we sat around the coffee table in the middle of my office. 'Before we start, what is happening with Sapphire Publishing and Robert Fielding?' he asked.

'Nothing. I haven't had time to look at the files on the USB he brought in. He said it contained the accounts, but I don't think it does. He knows there will be no sale until they grant probate on my father's estate. He seemed very interested, though.'

'Perhaps we should go over the files he gave to you as part of this investigation.' Ferdinand put out his hand, palm up, waiting for me to produce the USB out of thin air.

I tried to fill my pronounced sigh with indignation, but neither of them took any heed. The USB was still in my briefcase. I dug it out and gave it to Ferdinand.

'Seems odd to me that Mr Fielding would be interested in this business,' Ferdinand said, turning his laptop so that I could view the screen. 'There's not much in the way of assets. The building it works from — the offices, the furniture — are all leased from your father's mining company. The only tangible assets are the authors and the publishing rights to their books.'

'Are the bank statements on that USB?' I asked.

'No. Mr Fielding appears to be mostly interested in the authors your father had signed up.'

While we waited for Ferdinand to finish looking at the files, Sandy and I pored over the bank statements. Again. 'I think this is the definition of insanity,' I said aloud.

'What?' Sandy quizzed.

'Doing the same thing over and over again, expecting a different result.'

'What do you mean?'

'I've gone over these documents at least four times. Ferdinand has gone over them with his auditor's eye. My uncle has a copy of them. Nothing has changed; the money has gone.'

'We need to find out who took it,' Sandy grumbled.

'That isn't the question,' I said. 'It's more how did Steven get his hands on it? I'll make a time to visit my uncle. I think the three of us should go.'

'This is magnificent,' Ferdinand gushed when the front gates opened so I could drive into the property. 'What a marvellous garden. Who lives here again?'

'My uncle, his butler come bodyguard, and enough staff to run a small hotel.'

Ferdinand's mouth dropped open as we walked up the steps to the front door. Phillip opened it before I knocked, acknowledged me with a nod, and let his eyes wander quickly over Sandy before settling on Ferdinand. The frown that seemed to always crease his brow vanished, and a smile that I found a bit creepy spread over his face.

'Come in, gentlemen. Mr Warburton is in his office. This way.'

Phillip put his hand on Ferdinand's elbow and ushered him to my uncle's office. He left Sandy and I to find our own way.

'Just as well I've been here before,' I muttered. 'Might be left twiddling my thumbs in this entrance hall otherwise.'

Sandy poked me on the arm and told me to be quiet.

My uncle waited for introductions to Ferdinand and Sandy before offering anyone a seat.

'I have copies of the documents relating to the setting up of Sapphire Publishing,' he said, handing each of us an A4-sized stack of papers. 'Phillip, could you please ask Ally to get morning tea ready?'

He shut the door behind Phillip.

Ferdinand's gaze fixed on the door, as if he expected Phillip to materialise at any moment.

'Let us try to get our heads around what is going on before Phillip and Ally arrive with refreshments.'

Uncle Walton settled himself in his leather armchair and waited while the three of us organised ourselves. 'Money is missing. Lots of money. We will worry about how it came to be missing after we find out just how much. I'll let you start, Brad.'

I hate repetition; Uncle Walton knew how much money was missing, and I found it tedious to have to explain it again. Sandy poked me in the thigh with his index finger. I kicked his ankle.

'The cash at hand in Sapphire Publishing has gone from three million dollars to five hundred dollars. It appears Father's personal accounts are in order and have not been raided.'

'Yet,' my uncle interrupted. 'Your father's accounts are frozen until probate. Who is the executor of your father's estate?'

'His solicitor. The one who wrote his Will and squirreled away his money so that it was hard to steal. I wonder if Father did that after Steven started showing his true colours?'

'Give me the name of your father's solicitor. I will

chat to him or her and see if we can work together to get your parents' finances in order.' Uncle Walton flipped over some papers.

'Your poor father died on 15th June, and the last of the funds were taken from Sapphire Publishing on 31st July. Seems Steven didn't even wait long enough for the ink on the Coroner's Report to dry.'

'Before we all jump to obvious conclusions,' Sandy said, standing up – he always thought better on his feet – 'we have to prove Steven took all this money. And that's not our job.'

'Absolutely correct, Sandy. I should have added *alleged*,' my uncle said.

'I'm not adding *alleged* every time I blame Steven for this. He is the only one with the means and the knowledge to have taken the money.' I folded my arms across my chest like a petulant child, and glared at Sandy.

Ferdinand cleared his throat. 'I agree with Brad.'

A gentle tap on the door and Uncle Walton stood up. 'Come in.'

Phillip and a woman, presumably Ally, came in with a hotel room service trolley laden with tea, coffee, water, small sandwiches, petite fours, a fruit platter and cheese and biscuits on a cheeseboard.

'Goodness. You have gone to a lot of trouble,' Sandy remarked, salivating at the spread.

'Thank you, Ally. Lovely as usual.' My uncle held the door for the woman, and she left.

Phillip stayed. He poured coffee and tea and passed around plates and serviettes.

The refreshments done and dusted, Uncle Walton asked Phillip to show Ferdinand and Sandy around

The Betrayal of Ebony Makepeace

the house and the gardens. 'I want to chat to my nephew.'

'Are you sure it is Steven who has stolen this money?' he demanded as soon as we were alone. 'Your friend the detective is correct. It must be proven.'

'Who else would it be?' His rancour caught me off guard.

'You all seem to be quite adamant, without proof. I want to eliminate any other possibilities. What about Ferdinand? How trustworthy is he?'

I choked on my flat white. 'Uncle Walton, I trust Ferdinand with my life. The money started disappearing before Father died. Ferdinand is the one who pointed out the missing funds. He was preparing the Business Activity Statement because, well, who else would do it now the company is in limbo? Anyway, he's the type that if he came into money, he wouldn't be able to help himself. He would flaunt it shamelessly.'

'What about your friend?'

'My *friend* is more of a brother to me than Steven. And my friend, as clever a detective as he is, would not have the knowhow to take millions of dollars without being noticed. No. This has Steven written all over it.'

'Unless he is caught and still has money left, we will not recover these funds. You know that don't you, Brad?'

'Yes. I'm heartbroken for Father. On top of everything he went through, Steven has destroyed his passion.'

'Next steps?' my uncle asked.

'You speak to my father's solicitor, make sure his money is safe. I'll put some funds into Sapphire Publishing to make it more attractive for potential buyers.

By the way, one of my clients is interested. I'll give you his number, if you don't mind contacting him when you and Father's solicitor have probate.'

My uncle nodded. 'And...?'

'I'll get Ferdinand to liaise with you if there is anything else to report. For the time being I think we should leave things while we build a case for prosecution. I don't want Steven to know we are on to him.'

'I'm still not convinced it is him. See if your detective friend can get some proof.'

My uncle stood up and walked to the door when we heard the others in the foyer.

'Your knees don't seem to be as troublesome today, Uncle,' I said.

'No. It's wonderful. I've been using the exercise bike, and Phillip made an appointment for me at the orthopaedic surgeon, she drained out the fluid and injected cortisone into my knees. It's not a long term fix, but it is making life much easier while we work on these matters. I'll have surgery when we tie up this mess.'

Ferdinand's face was flushed pink, and his tie loosened a little when the three of them came back into the office.

'Did you enjoy the tour?' I asked.

'It's marvellous, just marvellous,' Ferdinand raved. 'You have a beautiful place here, Mr Warburton.'

'Thank you. Brad has decided you and I will liaise on the matters we discussed earlier, so perhaps you will visit again.'

I kept glancing at Ferdinand. He looked at Phillip, who smiled benevolently in Ferdie's direction. Sandy was oblivious. As I think, was my uncle. But who knows?

18

SANDY

Sandy followed Brad into the South Melbourne town house and picked up his car keys.

'Are you going?' Brad asked, concern creasing his brow and forming lines around the corners of his mouth.

'I planned to, yes. You know that worrying about all of this is giving you wrinkles, don't you?'

'Ah, there he is.' Brad moved behind the kitchen bench, filled the coffee machine, and turned it on. 'You might as well stay for a sandwich and a cup of coffee.'

Sandy put his keys down and pulled up a stool on the other side of the bench. 'We need to put a plan into action, don't we?'

Brad nodded; his usual bravado buried under apprehension. 'Where will I start?'

Sandy took the coffee Brad offered and sipped it a couple of times. 'In my opinion, you need to put "where is the money?" on the back burner and concentrate on what happened to your mother. Isn't that what started this whole journey?'

'What do you have in mind?'

'What type of security did your parents have at their house?'

Brad took bread out of the freezer and laid out four slices on the bench to thaw. 'Will one toasted sandwich be enough?'

'No. I'd like two, thanks. We had a big morning tea, but no lunch. I can't think on an empty stomach.' Sandy tapped his fingers on the bench while his friend put another two slices of bread out and asked if they were both for him.

'Yes. One sandwich will do me. I'm not hungry.'

'Back to the security,' Sandy nagged.

'They had a camera at the door. When you rang the bell, they could see who was there, and pressed a button to unlock the door if they chose, or to speak to the caller without opening the door.'

'Is this activity recorded?'

Brad peeled cheese slices off each other, cut up a tomato and open a jar of sliced pickled cucumbers. Sandy salivated.

'Yes. Why?'

'Back to the main point of our investigation — your mother! If Steven visited her, it would be recorded. No?'

'Yes. Father was particular about that, especially in those last few months.'

'Perhaps he didn't trust Steven around your mother.'

Brad turned his back on his friend to supervise the sandwiches in the sandwich maker. When they were ready, he passed a plate and napkin to Sandy, pulled up a stool next to him and waited while his friend took a bite of his sandwich.

'Didn't you have any ham?' Sandy asked, with his mouth full.

'No. Ebony is vegetarian. I don't buy processed meats. Any meats, for that matter. Processed meats are carcinogenic.'

'Oh, FFS. Where is she, anyway?'

'I don't know. Safe I hope.'

The friends ate the rest of their food in silence.

When they'd finished eating, Sandy continued the badgering. 'Get your notes, and we'll sit in the living room. You have to focus, Brad. Tell me how we get a copy of the recordings from the doorbell at your parents' house. We'll start the week before your mother died.'

Brad opened an app on his phone and sat next to Sandy who had set himself up on the couch in the family room. 'The recordings are listed here as messages. What made you think of this?'

'Seriously? I am a detective, my friend. I might not be in the Force any longer, but I'm still a detective. The recordings of visitors to the house is the first place to look. Why do you have the app? Would Steven have it too?'

'When Father had it installed, I was there, and he got the electrician to show us both how to get the app running. As far as I know Steven doesn't have it.'

Brad scrolled through the messages, saved as videos if someone rang the doorbell. The week before his mother died there were some deliveries, her brother Walton called in, and Steven, the night he said he found her dead on her bed.

'Uncle Walton didn't tell me he visited Mum that close to her death.'

'Bradley, Bradley, Bradley. We are not worried

about him right now. Steven rang the doorbell the night your mother died. You can see he let himself in, which means your mother didn't.'

Sandy leant back on the couch while his friend processed the information. He watched as the theories Brad had about his brother killing their mother morphed into possibilities and as they did, drained the colour from his face.

'I feel sick.'

Sandy poured Brad a glass of his favourite wine and put it in his hand. 'Drink.'

'It's likely Steven killed Mum, isn't it?' Brad croaked.

'Clutching at straws is not a good look on you. Was he there long enough? Doesn't the camera record goings and comings?'

Brad shrugged.

'Give me the damn phone.' Sandy scrolled through the photographs and videos on the app. 'Your father comes home before Steven leaves. He doesn't come in the front door, but through the garage. You can see his car in the driveway.' Sandy kept scrolling. 'Fifteen minutes after Steven lets himself in, paramedics arrive. Then police. Then the paramedics leave.'

'Why police?' Brad rubbed his eyes.

'The paramedics called them when they pronounced your mother deceased.'

'I don't understand. Wouldn't they take her body?'

'No, my friend. That's not how it works in Victoria. Ambulances don't carry bodies — unless a patient dies in transit, of course. When a death is unexplained – or sudden but not suspicious – like your mother's, the paramedics call the police. Police call the deceased's doctor to ask if they will issue a death certificate. Your mother's doctor must have said *no*, because someone from the coroner's office is on video at the front door. Which means, the police called them. If a doctor will issue a death certificate, police advise family or friends, whoever is there, to call a funeral director. It's not pleasant.'

'I didn't know that.' Brad stood and paced around the room. 'Father said he didn't go to Mum. Said he wanted to remember her as she was. He was lying, wasn't he?'

'Probably. Can't imagine arriving home to be told by your son that your wife is dead, and not going to her side.'

'Doesn't prove anything though, does it?' Brad looked at his friend with expectation etched on his face.

'No. Just proves Steven was there. Tomy will be able to get access to the triple zero call. That will tell us when Steven called an ambulance.'

'So now we have to prove that Mum was alive when Steven got there.'

Sandy sighed, stood up and went to the kitchen. 'I'm making coffee. Want one?'

19

BRAD

Sandy left about nine o'clock last night after I asked him to go. The day had taken a lot out of me, and as the wine, of which I drank too much, started working its magic, I wanted to go to bed.

The headache in the morning was as much from the wine as the stress. Coffee didn't help, but I drank two cups, anyway. While I was putting my briefcase on the passenger's seat, I noticed my shoes – they needed a polish. Why didn't I see that when I put them on? Best hide my feet under the desk if any clients come in. A random thought of how annoyed Ferdinand would be that my shoes were dusty, led to the vision of him swooning over Phillip at my uncle's the day before. 'Speak of the devil,' I muttered when his name popped up on my phone as an incoming call.

'Good morning,' he sang as soon as I answered.

'Is it?'

'Yes, grumble bum. It is. Are you on your way to the office?'

I looked at my shoes. 'One more quick thing to do, then I'm on my way.'

'Good. Your first appointment is at ten.'

'Last time I looked at my diary there wasn't anything until this afternoon.'

'Your father's solicitor wants to see you. I made a judgement call. And the right one, as usual.'

'Yes. Thank you. Be there soon.'

'What's happening to you?' Ferdinand snapped when I walked into the office.

'What are you babbling about?'

'You were polite on the phone. You were conciliatory when I announced the new appointment. Who are you, and what have you done with Bradley Culley?'

'Sometimes life just catches up,' I moaned. 'Are there any messages?'

'I've emailed them. Do you want a coffee?'

'No, thank you. I think I've overdosed on caffeine this morning.'

'There he is again. Where is Brad?'

I ignored Ferdinand's question and walked into my office. I had an hour before my father's solicitor arrived, and I needed to organise my thoughts.

Your ten o'clock is here, popped up on my computer screen.

'Shit. That hour went quickly.'

Ferdinand escorted a tall, clean-shaven, impeccably dressed older man into my office, and introduced us. 'Brad, this is Mr Shane Randell.'

I shook Randell's outstretched hand and offered him a seat. 'Would you like something to drink?' I asked.

'No. Thank you.'

On hearing the response, Ferdinand left, closing the door behind him.

'What can I do for you, Mr Randell?'

Randell put his briefcase on my desk, opened it and fossicked around for longer than the old Brad would have liked, and eventually pulled out a document.

'Your father's last Will and Testament,' he said, putting it in front of me.

I didn't reach out for the papers, didn't know how to react. My usual quick thinking brain was on vacation.

'Please take a look,' Randell said. 'I have a copy, too. I would like to go through it with you and explain some things.'

I picked up the document, leant back in my chair and started to read it before I realised Randell meant we were to go through it together. Oops.

'The first part of the Will is standard. He left everything to your mother, which is the norm. The next part explaining what is to happen if she predeceased him is more complicated.'

My eyes moved down to the paragraph where my mother's name was typed in bold. *If my wife, Wilhelmina Warburton/Culley, predeceases me, her share of my business, Sapphire Publishing, is to go to my eldest son, Steven Culley.*

I looked up when Randell finished reading. 'That doesn't surprise me,' I whined.

'It did me,' he said. 'I warned him you would have every right to contest that point in the Will, and that much of his estate would be lost in legal fees.'

'What did he say?'

'He told me to print it, he would sign it and take a copy.'

The new, brain-slow me, had no retort. Randell seemed genuinely surprised. Had he heard about my witty responses? I doubted it.

'Your father called me a few days after our meeting, and we arranged a clandestine sojourn at his brother-in-law's property in Macedon.'

'Uncle Walton,' I mumbled.

'Yes. Anyway, your father told your uncle and me that he was under duress when he wrote the first Will, and wanted a rewrite. We were sworn to secrecy, that we would not reveal the contents of a new Will he wanted to make, until it was probated.'

'Did my father explain what sort of duress he was under?'

'No. And neither of us asked.'

Randell fossicked around in his briefcase again and handed me another document of about four pages. 'This is his last Will and Testament. Your uncle has the original.'

'My head hurts,' I said aloud.

'It's a lot to take in,' Randell said, putting his briefcase on the floor.

'This is another piece of the puzzle that grows larger by the day. I don't understand why my uncle has not told me about this.'

'We agreed I would come to see you first. Something about you being distressed about your father's death at the hands of a police officer?'

A ruse. Clever Uncle Walton. Steven would stalk Father's solicitor, waiting for him to pay me a visit with the dreadful news that I was not getting a share in the publishing business.

'That was thoughtful of Uncle Walton. It has been a difficult few months, and Father's death was avoidable. What have you and my uncle been up to?'

Randell read through the new Will whilst I followed along. It was straightforward, written after Mum's death and after Steven had started to destroy Douglas Culley's life.

'You will notice,' Randell said, 'that you and your brother are to receive funds from the estate, after a donation to the Cancer Council. There is, however, a caveat on your brother having access to his share.'

I read the caveat. My poor father. I wiped my eyes while I read his attempt to punish Steven for destroying everything. 'Is this legal?' I asked.

'Yes. Quite. I believe your brother has skipped bail and can't be located? If it is proven that your brother threatened, manipulated, and otherwise dominated your father, he will not have access to the estate.'

I looked at the bottom right corner of my computer screen; it was quarter to twelve. 'Goodness, Mr Randell, I have kept you far too long. Thank you so much for bringing this to me and for working with my uncle. No doubt he will focus on probate, so we can get this all settled.'

'No doubt. If there is anything else I might help with, please let me know.' He handed me a business card.

After showing Randell to the elevator, I slunk back into my office and plonked onto one of the couches.

Ferdinand marched in and announced he was going to lunch. 'And I am going now before the real Bradley Culley returns.'

The real Bradley Culley was lost in the cosmos

somewhere with his broken heart. Broken first when his fifty-four-year-old mother died, second when his father committed suicide by cop, third when the brother he adored lost the plot, and last, when Ebony left him.

20

BRAD

Tomy's number came up on the phone's screen. 'Hello, Tomy. How's things?'

'Oh. I was after Brad Culley. This is his phone, isn't it?'

What is it with people expecting me to be rude and unpleasant? 'Hilarious. How are you?'

'Good. Sandy said you were under a bit of pressure of late. How are you holding up?'

The small talk would have sent the old Brad into a tailspin of witty, sarcastic retorts. This Brad couldn't be bothered. 'It's been hard. Getting there. What can I do for you?'

'Sophie Marris contacted me. She is trying to reach Ebony again, apparently.'

'What does she want?'

Tomy used her words wisely, concisely. No frills from this woman. 'I don't trust her. She said she wants to speak to Ebony about the book she's working on, but can't reach her. Asked me to speak to you.

Tomy knew Ebony wasn't living in the Altona house. She'd orchestrated Ebony's clandestine exit.

The Betrayal of Ebony Makepeace

But had Sandy told her Ebony, and I broke up? Probably. 'Don't you have Ebony's number?'

'She's not answering. It goes straight to voicemail. I've left a few messages, but she hasn't called back. Is she ignoring you, too?'

'Yes. Sadly. I have to trust she is safe. She fell off the radar when she got in your car.'

'Sophie Marris put the wind up her. I don't blame her for being scared. I'm sure she's fine. She will be in touch when she's ready.'

'Why haven't you arrested Marris? She's a crook. I reckon she knows where Steven is. Give me her number. I'll call her.'

'I would have her in a cell if I could prove anything. I can't yet. Be careful. Let Sandy know if you are meeting her. He should go too.'

The text with Sophie Marris's number popped up a few minutes after Tomy hung up.

Sophie Marris was quite resistant to meeting me instead of Ebony. She fell just short of tears when she begged me to reach out to Ebony.

'Have you two broken up?' she asked four times.

'No. And it's none of your business,' I said on the fourth occasion. 'Ebony is a writer. She wants time and space to write. What do you want?'

When she accepted my obstinance would not budge, she suggested we meet in a café near to my office. I called Sandy and gave him the details.

I told Ferdinand I was stepping out to see Sandy, which wasn't a complete lie. He grunted and mumbled loudly enough for me to understand that I should marry Sandy and get it over with. Apparently, we are perfect for each other. The old Brad would not have let that snide comment pass. This Brad ignored it.

The café wasn't one I'd been to, and I wondered how Ms Marris knew about it. I was early, but she had arrived before me and sat at a table in the middle of the room. Odd. I always preferred to sit around the edges. People pushed past and knocked you about if you sat in the middle. She nodded when she noticed me.

We sat in uncomfortable silence for a few moments. She asked me to come. I thought it apropos that she start the conversation. I waited. She stared.

'Is it table service?' The silence got the better of me.

'What? Oh, sorry. Yes, it is. They will be along shortly. I haven't ordered yet. Are you having anything to eat?' She pushed a menu across the table.

I decided on a cheese and tomato croissant and a flat white. Surely they can't do much wrong with that combination.

'Are you well?' she asked, after we'd given our orders to a trim young man in black pants and a bright pink shirt.

'Yes. Why?'

'I'm trying to start a conversation,' she said sulkily.

'I don't understand why you want to see me, so please excuse my reticence.'

'I don't want to see you, Mr Culley. I wanted to see

Ebony, or Sherryn, or whoever she is this week. But my approaches have been blocked.'

My skin prickled. 'Maybe she's playing games like my brother does.' I let that comment sit around the coffee mug she had just raised to her mouth. She put the mug down.

'Perhaps. My new employer is interested in her work and asked me to approach her with a view to a publishing meeting. Can you ask her if we can do that?'

The words wanted to spurt out of my mouth and into her face. They wanted to tell her to keep away from Ebony and me, and give Ebony the space she craved. But I controlled myself, like the new Brad that I was. 'No. She will contact you if she is interested in speaking about publishing her work. She is on a writers' retreat and enjoying her solitude.'

That was a good lie. Ms Marris seemed to go for that one. I would have to remember it. Quite believable. I don't know why it took me so long to come up with it.

Ms Marris didn't respond. She picked up a knife and fork and proceeded to eat a salad sandwich with the utensils. I stared at the croissant on my plate so she wouldn't see the look of disdain on my face. Who eats a salad sandwich with a knife and fork?

The croissant was burnt and the coffee cold. I wouldn't be hurrying back to this place. Most of the food stayed on my plate and the coffee congealed in my cup while it waited to be taken away.

'Not hungry?' she asked, wiping the remains of mayonnaise off her mouth.

'It was disgusting.'

'Oh, that's a shame. Mine was good.'

I let the comment slide. 'Well, looks like our conversation is over. Say hello to my brother for me. Tell him we are on to him and everything he has done, will you?'

Her face flushed. 'I don't see your brother. I don't know where he is.'

'Sure,' I said, pushing out my chair. 'I'll pay for mine at the counter.' I took in the sights and sounds of the café while I waited at the register to pay. Through the mirror behind the counter, you could see the street outside. My brother sat in the driver's seat of a dark blue, upmarket sedan. I put twenty dollars on the counter and walked towards the restrooms. Steven got out of the car.

My hands shook as I took the phone out of my pocket. My fingers would not obey my brain, so I told the Google assistant to call Sandy. 'Steven is in the street outside the café.' I heard the fear in my voice. 'I'm going out through the kitchen into the laneway at the back. It will have a laneway out the back, won't it? Please say yes.'

'Yes. They do at that end of town. Find somewhere safe, out of sight. I'll call Tomy.'

'I'll go into the lobby of one of the hotels.'

———

Ferdinand was on the phone when I lurched into the office. He told the person on the other end he would call them back.

'What's happened?' he asked, while I took some deep breaths.

'Steven sat in a car outside the café I went to. I evaded him. Detective Tomy is looking for him.' The fear was still in my voice. Anxiety gripped me around the throat.

'What café?'

'Does that matter?' I snapped.

'Yes. If it had been one of the nicer ones in the neighbourhood, you could have taken refuge there while you called for help. Instead, you had to run as if you were the fugitive.'

Ferdinand's reasoning baffled me. 'Ok. You can get back to your call. I'm all right, by the way.'

'I can see that.'

I walked into my office and closed the door behind me. Even with the thick glass that separated my office from reception where Ferdinand sat, I could hear him whining and complaining to the person on the other end of his call. Complaining that he didn't get to see him enough, and that if he cared about him, he would make the effort. Ferdinand's dramas would have to get in the queue if they wanted my attention.

21

SANDY

Sophie Marris and Steven Culley had vanished by the time Tomy arrived at the café. 'Which way did they go?' she asked Sandy.

'Into the traffic, heading north.'

'Why didn't you follow them?'

'My car is in the carpark of the office building I work in, Tomy. I no longer have access to the *police* signs to throw on the dashboard.'

'Sorry. I sometimes forget you are a civilian and not one of us anymore.'

'Thanks.' Sandy took his phone out of his pocket. 'It's Brad. We lost them,' he said into his mobile. 'Tomy got here too late and because I'm not in the Force anymore, I couldn't follow them.'

Tomy sneered at Sandy and grabbed his phone. 'I'm coming to see you. Are you at work?'

'Yes. I'm not going anywhere.'

'Good. Stay there.'

'Can I come too?' Sandy asked, sounding to himself like a petulant child.

'Sure. Sook. We'll take a real police car.'

Ferdinand was packing up for the day when Tomy

The Betrayal of Ebony Makepeace

and Sandy walked in. 'He's in his office. I'm going home. Let yourselves out.'

'What's up his nose?' Sandy asked Brad when he and Tomy took up their seats on the couch.

'He had a fight with someone this afternoon. On the phone. I caught the end of it when I came back from the Steven and Sophie rendezvous. I didn't have the energy to engage him, and he didn't offer an explanation.'

'So we won't be getting a latte then?' Sandy asked.

'No. I'm not making you one. There's a fridge in our kitchen. Help yourself to something from that, or make your own coffee.'

Sandy asked Tomy if she would like anything, ignored Brad, and made his way to the little kitchen.

'Why was Steven at the café?' Brad wanted answers from Tomy.

'Good question. Ms Marris would have told him Ebony wasn't available, and that you were meeting her. You seeing him there today is the proof we need to arrest her. But she got away, too.'

Sandy came back in holding a tray with three mugs and a plate of biscuits. 'Couldn't help myself,' he beamed. 'Where are we up to?'

'I was just about to ask Brad some questions.' Tomy picked up one of the mugs. 'Is there sugar in this?'

'There's one sugar in all of them. Take your pick.' Sandy passed a mug to Brad.

Tomy turned on the recorder on her phone and put it on the coffee table between the two couches. She identified herself, Brad and Sandy, and stated the time and date.

'I'm recording this, Mr Culley, so we don't miss anything. Are you ready?'

Brad nodded.

'Say your answer, Mr Culley.'

Sandy stepped toward Brad and put his hand on his shoulder before he complained about the rules. He knew his friend was struggling to cope.

'Why did you meet with Sophie Marris?' Tomy asked.

'She called, wanting to see Ebony again. I went instead. She said she wanted to work with Ebony to publish her books.'

'Mr Culley, did you suspect anything when you spoke to her?'

'Of course. Like you, I don't trust her. She kept glancing out the window, but I didn't follow her gaze. Stupid. I should have.'

'When did you first notice your brother, the fugitive, Steven Culley at the café?'

'When I was paying. I saw him through the mirror that was behind the counter. He stepped out of an upmarket sedan. I was too shocked to do anything but run.'

'Thank you, Mr Culley. Mr Sanderson will tell me what happened next.'

Tomy turned off the recorder on her phone and leant back on the couch. 'This is a shit show. Fancy being that close to Steven and not being able to apprehend him.'

Sandy noticed Brad fidgeting with the buttons on his jacket and that his right leg was constantly moving up and down. He sat on the couch next to him. 'What's wrong, Brad?'

'What? Oh. Nothing.'

'Bullshit. You're wound up like a toy train. You are staying at my place tonight.'

'You two make a lovely couple,' Tomy sniggered. 'I'm sorry you're feeling anxious, Brad, but there are more questions. Sandy says a solicitor came to see you. Randell? Tell me about him. Do you think he is on the level?'

'I'll have to look at my notes,' Brad said. 'My memory isn't good these days.'

He put his laptop on, well, his lap, and opened the lid. 'It will take a moment to warm up.'

'Like all of us,' Sandy said.

Looking over the notes he wrote after his meeting with Shane Randell, Brad shared all the information with Tomy and Sandy.

'I think we should put a tail on Mr Randell,' Tomy said. 'To see if he leads us anywhere.'

22

BRAD

I pulled up in the street outside the apartment building Ferdinand lived in, parking in a loading zone. 'I'm downstairs,' I said into my phone as soon as Ferdinand answered.

'On my way.'

'Don't you have anything better to do on a Sunday than spend it with me?' I said as I pulled onto the roadway.

'I'm not spending it with you. I am going to spend a lovely Sunday afternoon in the beautiful Macedon Ranges.'

'Hmm. Anything to do with Phillip?'

'Why? Is that a problem?'

I didn't answer. I didn't know what to say. Was it a problem? No doubt my uncle would tell me if it were. Something niggled at the back of my mind, though. The first time I saw Ferdinand and Phillip together, it seemed as if they'd met before. I had disregarded the thought as impossible, but the niggle hung around in my head. As annoying as it was, I didn't feel comfortable asking Ferdinand. Soon, though.

Ferdinand was uncommonly quiet during the trip

to my uncle's, and I had had so much going on in the last couple of weeks that I was glad of the silence, of not being pressured to make conversation. As I turned the car into the street that led to my uncle's, Ferdinand spoke.

'Thanks for bringing me along, Brad. I appreciate it. I don't get to leave the city much, and this is a lovely change of scenery.'

I wanted to quip that I was sure there would be more than scenery changing, but kept quiet. 'No worries. It's nice to clear the cobwebs.'

'See, there he is again. The nice Brad. When is the other one coming back? I want to know so I can prepare.'

Before I spoke, I took some deep breaths and gripped the steering wheel with my hands. 'I think, at this rate of badgering, he will be back sooner rather than later.'

Ferdinand sniggered. 'Yep, he's on the way.'

———

The gates magically opened when I pulled into the start of the driveway. Ferdinand grinned as if he had something to do with it. I parked on the other side of the circular drive and before I turned off the ignition, Ferdinand was closing the door and skipping up the steps to a waiting Phillip. I looked at them as I closed the driver's door and put the key fob in my pocket. Ferdinand almost launched himself at Phillip, who stepped back and said something I couldn't hear, before indicating to Ferdinand that he should go in the front door.

'Good afternoon, Mr Culley.'

'Good afternoon, Phillip. Please call me Brad.'

'Certainly. Your uncle is waiting on the back verandah. I'll organise refreshments.'

Phillip left me to my own devices. Any other time I'd come here, he escorted me to wherever I was supposed to go. I looked around the foyer for Ferdinand, but he was long gone, and Phillip disappeared quickly, too.

Before I stepped out on to the back verandah, I called out to Uncle Walton. Didn't want him to die of fright.

'Yes, Bradley, out here.'

I sat in the outdoor armchair my uncle pointed to and without waiting for the obligatory pleasantries to get out of the way, told him Shane Randell had been to see me.

He nodded. 'He said he was going to pay you a visit.'

'I have some questions,' I regaled my uncle.

He leant back and put his hands on the arms of his chair.

'Why didn't you tell me you visited Mother a few days before Steven is supposed to have found her body?'

I couldn't tell if he was amused, angry, or indifferent. His expression didn't change, but his stare bored holes through my forehead. I waited for him to ask me how I knew, but even though he was ten years older than Mum, he wasn't a technological Neanderthal. He didn't ask how I knew he'd visited my mother.

'She was my sister, Bradley. Am I not entitled to visit? Nothing untoward or sinister in my calling on her. We often had coffee together, but she called to say she didn't feel up to meeting at our favourite café, so I went to her.'

I waited for my uncle to continue. He didn't. But I needed more. 'Was she unwell? Do you think that had something to do with her death?'

'She complained about a headache. Your father had started behaving erratically, and it stressed her. Hindsight is a marvellous thing, Bradley.'

The vibes he emanated told me he didn't want to talk about it anymore, so I asked about Mr Randell. My uncle's body language changed into professional mode, if there is such a thing, and he crossed his feet over and told me to go ahead with my questions.

'Steven's influence on our father, for a start. And why didn't you tell me earlier about the latest Will?'

I heard footsteps heading our way and followed my uncle's lead in talking about the weather and the garden. One of my uncle's staff carried a tray with sandwiches and small cakes, which he placed on a coffee table between us. 'The coffee is coming, Walton,' the chap said, leaving us to partake of the goodies.

'You were about to say,' I said, before my uncle put up his hand to silence me. The coffee crept onto the verandah, supported by the same man.

When the help, or waiter, or butler, or servant, I had no idea what to call him, left, Uncle Walton poured a coffee into a small mug and handed it to me. He followed with a plate and a paper napkin.

Couldn't help myself. 'Paper napkin. My goodness, standards are slipping. Saves on laundry, I guess. Where is Phillip? Doesn't he usually look after your needs?'

'He does have some time off, Bradley.'

A curt *mind your own business about Phillip*.

We ate a sandwich and drank our coffee. I didn't hurry him; I'd observed enough to know he would restart the conversation when he felt it appropriate. He ran his index finger under his eye, followed by wiping it with a napkin before I realised he was wiping tears.

'If only I'd known how much stress your father was under, Brad.' (He called me Brad when I was being a good boy.) 'Steven was hell bent on destroying him and his publishing business, and in causing you and your lady friend harm. Where is she, by the way?'

I told him about the writers' retreat. He nodded and kept talking.

'Apart from your friend writing about Steven's environmental vandalism while he worked in the mining company, albeit unknowingly, Steven seemed to have an unreasonable hatred for Douglas.'

I knew all of this, wanted to look at my phone to see the time, and to hurry my uncle's meanderings. But I waited.

Your father asked me to contact Mr Randell surreptitiously because he thought Steven was watching him. Hence the birth of the new Will that Randell showed you. And yes. It is legal. It makes the previous one where Steven allocated all the assets to himself, null and void. Speaking of assets, Brad, we should talk privately at a different time about the Minors Trust Wilhelmina set up for you and Steven.'

23

BRAD

As if on cue, Phillip and Ferdinand appeared on the verandah. Even my uncle would have noticed something going on between the two of them.

I said goodbye to my uncle, thanked him for his hospitality, and told Ferdinand it was time for us to get back to the city. Phillip put his hand in the middle of Ferdinand's back and guided him into the house. I shook hands with Uncle Walton and Phillip and tried not to scrutinise Ferdinand's behaviour. He must have said his goodbyes to Phillip earlier, because he shook my uncle's hand and then shook Phillip's, thanking him for his company.

As the gates to my uncle's driveway closed behind us, Ferdinand started fidgeting with the sleeves on his cardigan. Was it a cardigan? What else would you call it? Note to self to ask him one day.

'Are you ok?' I asked, without taking my eyes off the road. It was early summer so the days were longer, a while before dusk, but I still didn't trust those ratbag kangaroos not to jump in front of the car.

'Is the new Brad still here?' Ferdinand's voice quivered.

'He is.'

'I really like coming up her to the Macedon Ranges. I'm reconsidering my life. That might mean leaving you.

'Oh.' Nothing else would come out of my mouth. I kept my lips pursed together in case a screech managed to escape.

'Thanks for your support.' Ferdinand stopped fidgeting and glared at me. I saw him out of the corner of my eye.

'I don't know what to say. It's up to you.'

We didn't speak again for the rest of the trip home. He thanked me when I dropped him off at his apartment block and said he would catch me in the morning. I surprised myself when I moved back into the traffic — I wasn't obsessing over Ferdinand's bombshell. Told myself it would sort itself out in due course. I had an urge to call Ebony to tell her about the new, unflappable me. Instead, I concentrated on the road, let myself into my townhouse and settled in for a Sunday evening of channel surfing.

Before I had finished my obligatory third cup of morning coffee, Sandy rang the doorbell. When I opened the door, he stepped inside, pushing me out of the way.

'Shit a brick, Sandy. Steady on.' My coffee spilt on the bamboo flooring.

'I'm sorry. Tomy asked me to speak to you.'

'It will have to wait until I clean up the mess.' I stomped into the kitchen, tore off some paper towel and looked daggers at him while I made my way back to the front door. Mess cleaned up, I sat on a stool at the bench with a fresh coffee in my hand. 'What is so urgent that you couldn't wait for me to invite you in like a civilised man?'

Sandy pulled up a bar stool next to me and asked if there was enough coffee for him. The old Brad would have sniggered and told him to make more if there wasn't, but the new Brad got off the stool, went to the cupboard, got out a lovely glass coffee mug, and filled it with freshly brewed coffee. That was enough, though. I told him to get his own milk and sugar.

'Some exciting news, Brad.'

I waited while he stirred his coffee.

'Tomy located Sophie Marris using her mobile phone pings.' He looked at me as if he didn't think I knew what he was talking about.

'And?' I shot him down in flames.

'Oh. You know what that means?'

'That question does not deserve an answer.'

'Oh. Ok. Anyway...'

'Wait.' I interrupted. 'Should a detective in the Victoria Police be sharing information with a civilian?'

Sandy's face coloured the red of an overripe tomato. 'No. She shouldn't, and normally wouldn't. But you and I and Ebony have a vested interest in the case, so she is telling me enough to keep me informed. She is withholding more than she's telling me. May I continue?'

I nodded.

'Sophie Marris's phone pinged at a phone tower near your parents' house.' Sandy paused – I assumed for dramatic effect. He sipped his coffee.

'What do you want me to say or do?' I snarled. 'You know that information is out of the blue.'

'Sorry. You are hard to read these days. I wonder if you've seen my old friend, Brad the Cad. When will he be back?'

I looked at my phone. 'It's getting on, it will be sunset before I even get to the office today.'

Sandy put his cup on the bench and said that Tomy had driven around the area in her own time and saw the car I had described in a driveway two doors up from my parents.

'How does she know it is near my parents?'

'She called me and asked if the area was familiar to me. I told her your parents' address.'

I felt sick. The coffee regurgitated into my throat. I struggled to get it back down. Sandy asked if I was ok, then cleared the cups.

'You should go to work,' he said. 'I came to fill you in, but there is nothing you or I can do until we hear from Tomy. We'll just get in the way.'

'That must be so hard for you.' I felt for Sandy. He left the job he loved because of what my brother had done to us all.

'Times like this it's hard. It's a case I know well. Never mind. It is what it is.'

'What will you do now?'

'Go to my office and try to get some work done. I have a new case. A missing young man the police don't have the time or the resources to follow up. One of those situations where the parents and friends fear foul play, but none of the evidence points to that.'

I grinned at my friend and told him I was happy he had a case to work on. 'Your business will grow. No doubt.'

'Thanks. I'll call you as soon as I hear from Tomy.'

The Betrayal of Ebony Makepeace

I arrived at the office before Ferdinand, so I called him. In all the years he had worked for me, the only time he wasn't at work before me was when he had COVID.

'Are you ok?' I asked when he answered.

'Sure. I overslept. Sorry. Be there soon.'

He ended the call before I had a chance to tell him not to hurry, to take his time. His relationship with Phillip still niggled at the back of my mind. I was missing something.

A barrage of emails hit me when I launched the program, but the only one of interest hailed from Uncle Walton. He'd written it not long after Ferdinand and I left yesterday, and sent it to my new Gmail account. As I was about to open it, Sandy called.

'They've arrested your brother. Along with Sophie Marris.'

Sandy didn't add anything else. He waited for that information to settle in my brain.

'At the house near Mum's?'

'Yes. Hiding in plain sight. They'd been there since he skipped bail. I'll let Tomy fill you in on all the details. She is yet to tell them to me.'

I leant back in my chair and put my hand over my heart. It hadn't raced like this since Steven kidnapped me. Did I need coffee? No. I made a cup of French Earl Grey tea, and while my shaking hands picked up the cup, I felt tears running down my cheeks. Although I knew the dramas that consumed my life weren't over, the arrest of Steven released bottled up anxiety that had been festering in my soul.

I sat at my desk, hot cup of tea in hand, and

opened my uncle's email just as Ferdinand walked in. He looked dishevelled, something he never did. I waved, and he nodded his head and made his way to the kitchenette. He would speak when he was ready.

> *Dear Brad.*
>
> *It was lovely to see you again today. There is information I wish to share with you, but didn't want to do so while we had company. I am in the city on Wednesday morning next week. Are you able to meet me somewhere quiet? We can have lunch. I suggest the Melbourne Club. I will email you a pass so you can park in the underground car park. I'll see you in the dining room at 12.30 if that's convenient.*
>
> *Let me know.*
> *Uncle Walton.*

The old me would have called him, or emailed back wanting to know why the cloak and dagger routine, but the new me was more perceptive and picked up that all was not well.

> *Hi Uncle Walton.*
> *Sounds lovely. I'll see you then.*
> *Brad.*

Nothing to be done. I would have to wait until next week.

24

EBONY

Ebony finished her walk around Lake Wendouree and looked at the fitness tracker on her wrist. She had completed the six kilometre circuit in thirty-seven minutes. 'Well, what a turnaround,' she said to the piece of technology. 'It took me an hour when I first started.'

Pleased with her efforts, Ebony stood looking over the expanse of the lake, watching the ducks and swans prepare for the oncoming twilight. She lived on the wrong side of the lake to see the sunset, but sometimes made the effort to make sure she walked at the right time. Today she was happy to get such a good walk under her belt.

Bidding goodnight to the water birds, she made the way to her cottage. She had been living here for six months, had not heard from Brad, and was surprised he respected her wishes and didn't badger her.

Sniffing under her arms, she decided a shower was in order, after which she put on a lightweight pair of three-quarter pants, t-shirt, and sandals. While she was making a coffee with the capsule machine that came with the cottage, she felt an overwhelming urge to call Brad. She shoved the urge back down into her gut.

Dinner wasn't a priority this evening, so Ebony turned on the television to watch the news. With coffee spilling down the front of her clean white t-shirt, she gasped at the lead item. Steven Culley and his accomplice, Sophie Marris, had been arrested.

Ebony thumped down on the couch and took deep breaths to slow her heart rate. The pounding in her ears took over her surroundings, so she turned up the television. *The fugitive, who was on bail when he disappeared, had been living two doors down from his deceased parents' house. In plain sight of Victoria Police. His accomplice, Sophie Marris had liaised with police while she was keeping Culley hidden.*

Ebony looked at her phone, expecting it to ring. She thought Brad would make contact now his brother was again in custody. Nothing.

The discomfort from the spilt coffee brought her mind back to the mundane. She went into the bedroom and changed her top, running shirtless into the living room, when her mobile rang.

'Brad. I saw it on the news. Are you ok?' Ebony hadn't waited for Brad to speak.

'Yes. I'm fine. Wasn't sure if my call would be welcome.'

'I've been thinking about you for a few days. Thinking about calling you. Then the news. I would have called if you didn't get in first.'

'Good to know.' Brad sighed into the phone. 'It's all been a bit much, to be honest. Lots to sort through.'

Ebony waited for Brad to ask her if she was going home. He didn't. 'I'm coming home, Brad. I'll leave at the end of the week. Coincidentally I have already given notice.'

Ebony unlocked the front door of the Altona townhouse, tapped in the alarm code, and closed the door behind her. She stood still for a few moments, taking stock of what she was about to do. Telling herself she was ready to return to the life she was trying hard to establish before Steven Culley got in the way. She parked her suitcase at the foot of the stairs and made her way to the kitchen, resigning herself to the fact that the first cup of coffee would be black. She would have to go to the supermarket.

Looking around the living space, she could see Brad had not stayed there since she left. The place was almost as she left it. Almost. She expected to be able to write her name in the dust on the coffee table. Instead, it sparkled, as did the other hard surfaces in the room. The rug showed the up and down strokes of a vacuum cleaner, and the drapes were open to let in the sun as it made its way to the west. She smiled. Brad either cleaned, or had someone come in to clean. 'I wonder?' she said, walking towards the fridge. It was stocked with butter, eggs, soy milk, soy yoghurt, a litre carton of cow's milk, and carrots, pumpkin, and sweet potato in the crisper. Her favourite plant-based foods were in the freezer. Ebony opened the pantry door and found it equally well supplied.

'He is a very thoughtful man,' she said, putting the kettle on.

Ebony took her suitcase up to her bedroom and found crisp, clean sheets on the bed, a new duvet cover, clean towels in the ensuite, and the furniture as dust free as the living room.

She took her clothes out of the suitcase and put them away in the wardrobe and drawers, where they used to live. She changed into a lightweight tracksuit she had bought when in Ballarat and went downstairs to drink her much needed coffee.

Ebony dozed on the couch while the events of the last year ran through her head like a movie reel. The buzz of her phone startled her back to the present. Expecting it to be Brad, she swiped the screen to accept the call without looking at it.

'I've been waiting for your call.'

'That is wonderful,' the female voice chirruped. 'I'm from Telstra and I'm calling about your internet. We've noticed it's not working properly.'

If Ebony hadn't been so tired, she would have espoused such vitriol into the mouthpiece the woman's ears would have burnt. Instead she hung up and blocked the number. 'They'll use a different number next time. Bastard scammers.'

While Ebony was waiting for the toasting process to finish on two slices of bread, she broke two eggs into a frypan. 'I am hungry,' she said to the eggs as she flipped them onto the toast. 'Do you know why Brad hasn't called me?' she asked the food, before she put her knife and fork into the egg yolks.

No response.

25

BRAD

It was killing me not to call Ebony. When she said she would be home at the end of the week, I stocked the fridge and pantry with essentials and hired a cleaning company to spruce the place up. You could write your name in the dust on the coffee table and the television screen. The place was cold too. Ebony had been away for most of autumn and all of winter; even though the days were warmer now, it seemed to take a long time for the bones of the Altona townhouse to thaw out and heat up. I looked online and found a local company to service the split systems in the house: one large one downstairs and three smaller ones upstairs. I turned them all on for the couple of hours I was sorting out the food requirements. Made a difference. I topped up my thoughtfulness with a beautiful bouquet of native flowers in a vase in the centre of the dining table. Although I knew the little things that would make her happy, I would not call Ebony first. I would wait for her to reach out to me.

I knew she was back. When she opened the front door and keyed in the alarm code, the app on my phone had a little stress attack. It had been a while. She didn't call me when she got home, even though she would have been impressed and grateful for the lengths I had gone to, to make the house clean and welcoming. Maybe she was tired.

She didn't call me until lunchtime the next day.

'Hi,' I said lamely when I answered. 'How are you?' My conversation skills were slipping.

'Hi, Brad. Thank you so much for preparing the townhouse for my return. It looks lovely. The flowers, the cleaning, the food. I appreciate it.'

'You'd been gone a while. It needed some TLC.'

'Would you like to come over for dinner? I have lots to tell you, and I'm sure you have had a lot going on in your life, too.'

I took a deep breath. Where was this going? I decided not to ask questions, but to accept the invitation. I told Ebony I would be there around six-thirty. She said she was looking forward to seeing me and hung up before I could respond. Just as well. I didn't know what to say.

It was early summer, and the Esplanade was busy with visitors lobbing into Altona for picnics on the beach. As annoying as it could be, the local traders relied on the business. There were no car spaces outside the townhouse, so I parked in a "no standing" spot on the other side of the road from Ebony's and called her.

'Hi. Everything ok?' she asked.

'Yes. All good.' There were those wonderful conversation skills again. 'May I park in the garage? There's nowhere left on the street.'

'Sure. Are you nearby?'

'Over the road.'

The door opened, I checked for traffic, then pulled into the garage where my SUV would be safe.

Ebony opened the door that led to the house and waited for me to close the garage door and step toward her. 'Come in. I've got some nibbles and drinks ready.'

The skin on my arms tingled and butterflies flapped around in my gut. I hadn't seen her in over six months. She looked more beautiful than ever. The old Brad wanted to ravish her, to pull her into him, to kiss her, fondle her, to throw her on the couch and let six months of stress find a release. He wasn't around. The new Brad told Ebony how lovely she looked, how relaxed and happy, and how hungry he was. She frowned a little and turned her head on the side like a confused puppy. Ferdinand mustn't have sent her the memo about the new Brad.

'Let's sit down and have a drink,' she said. 'We know each other well enough not to pretend with the forced niceties.'

What a relief.

'Dinner smells good,' I said, taking up the position indicated on the couch.

'I learnt some new recipes while I was away. Thought I'd experiment on you,' she said, the corners of her mouth going up into that endearing half smile. 'By the way, where did you tell people I'd gone?'

'I said you were on a writers' retreat. Everyone I said that too, seemed to believe me. So either that is something they would expect of you, or I'm a bloody good liar.'

'Let's hope it's the former.' Ebony offered me the charcuterie board and a napkin.

We didn't speak much for a while. We sipped the wine, nibbled on the treats, and tried to relax in each other's company. I broke the silence. 'I missed you.' There, said it and to hell with the consequences.

'I missed you, too. But considering the start we had, and all the other dramas that befell us, we needed a break.'

I disagreed. But nodded as if she were the most knowing sage on the planet.

'Tell me about your brother and Sophie Marris. I must admit it surprised me to see she was with him.'

I told Ebony about the meeting I had with Sophie Marris at the café and of spotting Steven in the street. 'It was the description of his car I gave to Tomy that brought him undone.'

'How so?'

Apparently she gained access to the CCTV footage in the area, identified the car, secured the number plate, and tracked the vehicle to the house just down from my parents' place.'

'Wow! That's incredible. Well done, you. It must have been scary, seeing him.'

'I nearly soiled myself I was so shocked.'

Ebony leant over the coffee table and patted my knee. 'I can imagine.'

Her Amazon Echo chirped an alarm, which saw Ebony jump to her feet and head to the kitchen. 'Alexa, stop.' The alarm petered into silence. 'If only everything in our lives was that easy to manage,' she said, setting the plates out on the bench.

'When did you get that?' I asked, pouring us each a fresh glass of wine.

'I bought it while I was at my retreat.' She grinned. 'I use it for a range of stuff, and I'm learning to access it more each day. You should get one.'

'I've got enough people to yell at in my day without yelling at yet another screen.'

Ebony put a large pie in the centre of the table with bowls of vegies whose range of colours made one feel joyous: baby carrots, broccolini, sweet potato crisps, baby peas, sweet corn. I salivated. 'This looks amazing. What sort of pie is it?'

'I'll tell you later. I don't want you to bite into it with pre-conceived ideas.'

I would have preferred to be told, but Ebony was in charge.

The large slice of pie sat in the centre of my plate, and I surrounded it with a little of each of the vegetables. 'Do I need tomato sauce?'

'Why not taste it first?'

I could tell the pie-filling was the plant-based mince that I liked, and Ebony had flavoured it with tomatoes, onions, and a range of herbs and spices, of which garlic was the standout.

'No tomato sauce?' she said, reaching for the last of the broccolini.

'You know me well.'

I cleared the table and stacked the dishwasher while Ebony put the uneaten vegetables and pie in containers and into the fridge.

She invited me to sit on the couch while she made coffee. She put mine on the coffee table in front of me, and carefully balanced hers in her hand while sitting herself down alongside me.

'Tell me all the details about Steven's capture. All of it. And I want to know how it has all affected you.'

Because I wasn't sure where our relationship was going, whether this was a "friend" thing, or a "real" thing, I was selective in the telling of events. I told her Steven appeared to have embezzled from Sapphire Publishing.

'Oh. That's disappointing,' she huffed. 'I am ready to submit a new manuscript, and I was hoping to send it to them.'

'You still can. I put money into the business because we have an interested buyer. Not a good look when the bank accounts are empty.' I gulped my coffee. I'd let it cool down too much while I told her the stories.

'You are a marvel, Brad,' Ebony said, moving closer to me. 'Am I being presumptuous by sitting here?'

I crossed my legs. It had been quite some time. I hadn't been with anyone since Ebony left, and thinking about undoing the buttons on her shirt and holding her breasts made me literally ache with desire. But I played it cool, wanting to make sure I was reading the signs correctly. I squeezed my thighs together. 'I don't want to read something that isn't there,' I said to her.

'It's there, all right. If you are still interested in me. Going away for those six months was the best thing I could have done for myself and for our relationship. I am ready to rebuild what we had, but slowly, if that's agreeable to you.'

Agreeable? My poor aching, throbbing penis was ready to burst, but lust would have to wait. She would look for tenderness and understanding. 'We can play it by ear and see how things go, if you like,' I said. Restraint was a hard skill to manage in such circumstances.

'You can uncross your legs,' she said, winking. 'I know you well.'

She stood in front of me, unbuttoning her shirt, which fell to the floor, revealing the breasts I had dreamt about. She pulled down her three-quarter pants and stepped out of them. By the time I realised what colour her undies were, they too were on the floor.

'Your turn. I'll help.'

When the restrictive clothing was removed from my person, she straddled my legs, and guided my throbbing, aching body part into her. It had been a long time.

'Are you staying the night?' she asked when we were both spent, but she was still sitting on top of me.

'Yes, please.'

26

SANDY

Sandy waited in the foyer of the Victoria Police building in Spencer Street while the officer on the desk let Tomy know he was there.

'She is sending someone to escort you to her office,' she snarled in Sandy's direction. 'Wait over there.' She pointed to a row of seats lined up in front of the window.

Sandy moved toward the seats, but remained standing. When he was in the Force, this officer would have spoken to him with deference to his position. A position he no longer had.

'This way, Mr Sanderson,' the young constable said, as he stepped out of the elevator.

'Thank you. I can find it myself. I worked here for a long time,' he grumbled so the constable could hear him.

'So I believe. But you no longer do, so I will treat you as if you are a regular member of the public. Which you now are.'

Sandy bit his tongue. He didn't want dramas every time he came to Tomy's office. *Police have long memories.*

'Thanks, Constable. All good.' Tomy dismissed the young man with the wave of her arm. 'Let's go into the meeting room and chat,' she said to Sandy before he spoke.

Tomy closed the meeting room door and Sandy found a seat at the end of the table. She sat next to him.

'Big room for two little people.' He grinned.

'The walls have ears, and I have been told to be selective about what I share with you. Guess *they* think we are still friends, and I might say something I shouldn't.'

'That's insulting, Tomy. You wouldn't share information willy-nilly.'

She shrugged her shoulders. 'Ok. Here's what I can tell you. We charged Steven Culley with the kidnap and assault of his brother, and for breaking his bail conditions.' Tomy's eyes locked onto Sandy's face.

'I'm aware. We charged him with kidnap and assault before he disappeared. What else?'

'That's it at the moment.'

'What about embezzlement? What about the manipulation of his father?'

Sandy got up and paced the room. Tomy took in a deep breath and asked her friend to sit down. 'Forensic accountants are working with Brad's uncle. Do you know him? Walton Warburton? What is it with a name like that? What were his parents thinking?'

'Buggered if I know.' Sandy didn't hide his annoyance. 'What about Brad's mother?'

'Mrs Culley was dead when Steven arrived at the house. We've checked all the security footage and his phone records. He was in the house six minutes before he called an ambulance. If he had killed her, it would have taken longer than that to do the deed, secure the site to ensure it looked natural, and make the call. The autopsy clearly showed she died of a brain aneurism.

'It happens, Sandy. It happened to an aunt of mine. She said she had a headache, went to lie down, and never woke up.'

'What have you told Brad?'

'Nothing yet. Will do so soon. You should never have resigned, Sandy. This private detective stuff doesn't suit you. You're missing all the fun.'

Sandy ignored her comment. 'Treat me like the civilian your colleagues are fond of doing, and explain it all to me. At least the parts you are allowed to share.'

'There is not much more to add. Steven rented the house two doors up from his parents' house before he kidnapped Brad. We don't know why yet. He used an alias, of course. It was his base while he was tormenting his father and brother, and while trying to get rid of Ebony Makepeace. That story she wrote really put the wind up him. Far too close to the bone.'

'What about Sophie Marris?'

'Accessory before the fact right now. That's enough to hold her. We've successfully challenged her argument for bail. She is in custody.'

'Before what fact?' Frustration tinged Sandy's voice.

'Before Steven kidnapped and assaulted Brad. Lots to unpack. Not at liberty to say any more.'

'Thanks for seeing me. I know how busy you are,' Sandy said, giving Tomy a hug. 'You should catch up with Brad and me at Claude's one night.'

'That would be great. Text me when.' Tomy walked

to the elevator with Sandy, blowing him a kiss as the doors closed.

Walking back to his office gave him the opportunity to process the snippets Tomy had deemed appropriate to share. Compartmentalising the information into the appropriate storage areas of his brain, he sat at his desk, turned on his laptop, and typed up some notes ready to share with Brad.

27

BRAD

My uncle had emailed me a parking pass and a guest tag for the Melbourne Club. I shouldn't have been surprised to learn he was a member, as was my grandfather before him. My dear grandfather had taken me to the Club for my eighteenth birthday. Which was six months before he died.

The concierge scanned my pass with a phone, checked all was in order, and smiled the benevolent smile of someone whose station in life is higher than your own, as he pointed me toward the dining room. The old Brad would have sniggered, been asked to leave, and been embarrassed. The new Brad thanked the man and trotted off.

Uncle Walton saw me walk into the room and waved me over to his table. I noticed he pushed himself up using the arms of the chair. *The knees must be playing up again.*

'Glad you could make it, Brad. Is the location of this table all right?'

'It's fine, Uncle Walton.' I looked at the sumptuous surroundings, the perfectly set tables with crisp white linen, the smell of wealth and privilege oozing from every surface. This is the world in which my mother grew up.

'I think we will order before we start our conversation if that's ok?'

Something wasn't sitting right with me. My uncle had asked me twice if his decisions were acceptable, but I kept my concern to myself, nodded, and looked over the menu. I wasn't hungry until I saw the list of fare available.

'What would you like, Brad?'

'I'll have the oysters for entrée,' (I could hear Ebony in my ear, complaining that I'd fallen back into my carnivorous ways), 'and the pesto pasta for main.'

'Are you sure? There is an extensive menu. Why don't you have the rib eye?'

Silly as it was, I didn't want to tell my uncle that Ebony's influence on my diet, as well as most other things in my life, was extensive.

'I feel like pasta, Uncle Walton. Is that all right?'

He nodded and gave the waiter my order before sharing his. He ordered salmon for entrée and rib eye for main. I pondered changing my order because I was worried I would salivate watching him eat his steak.

The waiter poured a French Bordeaux into our glasses and left us in peace.

'Let's get started,' he said, as soon as the waiter left. 'It's wonderful that Steven has finally been caught. Do you know what the charges are?'

'To be honest, Uncle, I haven't followed up. I could find out from the detective on the case, but I'm not feeling inclined.'

'Irrelevant for our purposes, anyway. So we can get back to it.'

Uncle Walton pulled his laptop out of the bag he

had on the floor and cleared a space on the table. 'Do you want to sit around here so we can both see the screen?'

I sat in the chair nearer to him, and he put the laptop between us.

'What am I looking at?' I asked.

'I'll explain as we go along, but for starters, we are still investigating Steven in relation to the embezzlement of funds from Sapphire Publishing. But that isn't why I asked you here today. The Minors Trust your mother set up for you and your brother.' He stopped speaking and looked at me for a response. I nodded. 'It's empty.'

The glass that was making its way to my mouth went back to the table. 'What do you mean, it's empty?'

'You were about to have a drink. Follow through.'

I picked up the glass and swallowed a mouthful of the French wine. It slid down my throat like a piece of silk and instantly made me feel better.

'It's good, isn't it?' My uncle took a mouthful.

I nodded.

I looked at the computer screen. The figures formed a pattern: the first withdrawal was a month after my father died, and subsequent withdrawals were at fortnightly intervals. 'What's going on? More of Steven's handiwork?'

'Look at how the money was withdrawn. Not all at once. Someone who knows how to navigate the financial sector without raising alarm bells, set this up. I don't think Steven has that kind of knowledge. Do you?'

'No. He would have taken funds out in bigger

amounts, and on fewer occasions, like he did with the publishing company.'

'Yes. Which would have attracted attention. Your office has audited this fund since your mother died. You do know that, don't you?'

I put the glass on the table before my shaking hand spilt the expensive contents on the perfect, crisp, white tablecloth.

'Brad?'

The entrées arrived. We both waited while they put the food in front of us. Well, Uncle Walton's was put in front of him. Mine went to the place setting where I was supposed to be seated.

I kept quiet until the waiter was out of earshot before I answered my uncle. 'Before Mother died, you handled it. This doesn't prove my office is involved in the disappearance of the money.' I was clutching at straws.

'Yes. I did. An auditing firm the family had used for years managed it. But your father suggested giving it to you to manage after Mina passed away. The money disappeared on your watch. You know what this means, Brad?'

'Yes.' I pushed the oysters away and beat myself up about the waste of food and that the creatures' lives were lost in vain. 'We should have waited until after we finished our lunch to look at that information.'

'Perhaps. But I believe good food helps one put their thoughts in order. So I would encourage you to eat the oysters, and then your pasta. We can retire to the lounge with coffee and continue our chat after we've eaten.'

Despite myself, the oysters were delicious. I can

only imagine how much more delicious they would be if one were in the right frame of mind.

The pasta, full of flavour and cooked perfectly, was easy to eat. I pushed the dread out of my stomach long enough for the meal to settle.

'What am I supposed to do?' I asked my uncle while we moved into the lounge room and took up an armchair each.

'With your agreement, I will ask the auditors we engaged originally to use their forensic accountant to go over the Trust's records. We will leave things be until we hear from them.'

'Is this what you couldn't tell me at the weekend?' I asked, knowing the answer.

He nodded. 'Phillip is quite enamoured with your Ferdinand. For the first time in all the years he has been with me, I wasn't able to share a confidence with him.'

'Is Ferdinand responsible?' The panicked thoughts of running the business without him took second place to the shock and disbelief that he would betray me.

'Seems so. He is the auditor. He had the means. As hard as it is going to be, pretend all is well. We can't proceed until the forensic accountant and auditor have evidence. Drink your coffee. You look as if you need it.'

I sat in the car for at least thirty minutes, processing the information Uncle Walton had given me. I would struggle with "business as usual" with Ferdinand.

Telling myself that we didn't have any firm evidence yet, made it easier.

I walked into the office with my phone to my ear, pretending I was talking to Sandy, so I didn't have to speak to Ferdinand. He snarled and returned his gaze to his computer screen.

I closed my office door just in time to see Ebony's name come up on my phone's screen.

'Hi,' she chirped into the phone. 'How was your lunch with your uncle?'

'Lunch was fine. It was what he had to say to me that has shattered my world.' I waited the few seconds I knew Ebony would need to process my answer.

'It sounds distressing. I have banana bread in the oven, and am whipping up some hamburgers for dinner. Yes, the plant-based ones. Goes without saying. Close up shop and come over now. We will eat and you can talk.'

'I have some work to do for a client before I leave. I'll be there around 5.30, traffic permitting.'

'If you leave now, traffic will permit, and you can do your client's work from here.'

'You know that won't happen, Ebony.' I tried to sound flippant, but my distress dragged down my voice and my emotions. She picked up my mood and told me to get there when I could.

I jumped with fright when Ferdinand opened my office door and walked in. My client's work had kept my mind off lunch with my uncle.

'I'm leaving,' he said, a little more acerbic than usual.

I looked at the time on my laptop. 'Oh, shit! Didn't know it was that late. See you tomorrow.'

Ferdinand frowned. 'Is old Brad on his way back?'

'I think so,' I said, willing my voice not to quiver.

'Of course he is. *She* must have returned from the dead.' Ferdinand left my office door open when he walked out.

I called Ebony to let her know I was on my way.

28

SANDY

For the first time ever, Sandy arrived at Claude's before Brad. He opted for a table in a quiet corner and ordered bruschetta and two beers to be brought to the table when Brad arrived. He didn't wait long.

'Ordered anything?' Brad asked, after shaking his friend's hand.

'Yes. On its way.'

'You are scaring me with that face. Uncle Walton had the same face last week when I met him for lunch. He had bad news. Do you have bad news?'

Sandy's brow creased and he shook his head slightly. Brad waited.

The drinks were put in front of them, and the bruschetta sat in the middle of the table.

'Would you like to order anything else?' the waiter asked.

'I'll let you know,' Sandy said, taking the lead.

'Ebony is back.' Brad sipped his beer.

'Do you know where she has been for the last six months?'

'No. She'll tell me if she wants to. My fear, or guess,

or hunch, is that she's keeping it a secret in case she wants to run off again to the same place.'

'Maybe.' Sandy took a slice of bruschetta. 'Have a piece. It's good.'

Brad obeyed his friend. 'Get on with your story. I'm on edge enough.'

Sandy filled Brad in on the information Tomy had given him. Watching his friend's face as he absorbed some and struggled to deal with the rest, Sandy felt sick for him. 'There's more,' he said, when Brad looked into his eyes. 'Ferdinand is in a relationship with Phillip, your uncle's assistant.'

Brad jumped up from the table and sped to the bathroom. Sandy waited.

'Ok?' he asked when Brad came back.

'What a waste of a good beer,' Brad mumbled, wiping his brow with the back of his hand. 'How did you find out about Ferdinand? And what else do you know? I suspected something between the two of them. And my uncle has suspicions, too.'

'Your uncle and I had a chat over the phone last week, and he told me Phillip was seeing Ferdinand. Phillip has a cottage on the grounds. Did you know that?'

Brad nodded his head. 'Relevance?'

'None. I suppose. It's just that he kept Ferdinand's visits secret because they were in the cottage. Ferdinand stayed clear of the house.'

'How did he get to Macedon? He doesn't have a car. I took him a couple of times.'

'Train to Woodend. Phillip collected him from there.'

'Secretive little shit.' Brad shook his head when the waiter asked if they wanted to order a meal. 'Did my uncle tell you about the disappearing money from the Trust?'

'No. What's happened?'

'My uncle has forensic accountants and auditors looking into it. He suspects Ferdinand.'

It was Sandy's turn for the colour to run from his face. 'Not Steven?'

'Apparently not. He probably embezzled from Sapphire Publishing, but not the Trust.'

'Shit, Brad. That's awful.'

'You have something else to tell me. Out with it.'

'Steven was telling the truth about your mother's death. She was deceased when he arrived at the house.'

'I'm not convinced. And never will be. He certainly hastened Father's death. What is happening with that as far as charges go?'

'I don't know, Brad. Tomy wouldn't, couldn't share the details of the case with me. Suffice to say he is being charged with kidnap and assault – of you – of course. I asked if he was being charged with break and enter and criminal damage of your place in South Melbourne, but you didn't put in a police report. Did you?'

'No. Didn't see the point at the time. What's happening with that manipulative Sophie Marris?'

'They have charged her with being an *accessory before the fact*.'

'I don't know what that means,'

Sandy sighed, worried that his friend was having trouble focussing. 'They allege she knew Steven was going to hurt you, at the very least.'

'Thanks. You've been a great support, as usual. I'm going home to Ebony.'

29

BRAD

In the week since Sandy and I caught up at Claude's and he filled me in on some details surrounding Steven and Sophie Marris and Ferdinand, I had barely slept. Going to the office each day and pretending to be the flippant, self-assured arsehole I was normally, took all my strength. Going home to Ebony each night was the only thing that kept me sane.

The office was locked when I got out of the elevator. Ferdinand wasn't sitting at his desk, no lights were on. It had been so long since I was the first to open the office that I had to check the notes in my phone for the alarm code. I stood in the centre of the reception space wondering what I should do first. Flicking on the light switch near the door illuminated the entire office: reception, the kitchen, my office, the meeting room. Seeing the light on in the kitchen prompted me to wander in and put on the kettle. I filled it up with water, and filled up the coffee machine with fresh water, got the container out of the cupboard, and topped up the coffee bean receptacle. After checking the fridge to see if there was any milk, I made myself a latte and took it to my desk. Just as I plugged in the laptop and turned it on, my mobile rang.

'Good morning, Uncle Walton.'

'Hello, Brad. Are you at the office?'

'Yes. Why?'

'Is Ferdinand there?'

'No.'

'Oh. I see. I was going to call you yesterday, but I didn't have the authority. Today, I do. The forensic accountants passed on their findings to Victoria Police, and to me. It will depend on the police investigation, but the forensic accountants are recommending Ferdinand be charged under Division 2 of the Crimes Act 1958.'

'What does that mean, Uncle Walton? I'm overwhelmed with it all.'

'I'm sorry, Brad. The recommended charges are false accounting (section 83) and falsification of documents (section 83A).'

I had drunk half the coffee before my uncle called, and now it threatened to make its way up my gullet and onto my desk. I told Uncle Walton I would call him back.

Kneeling over the toilet bowl watching the coffee, milk, and Vegemite toast I had for breakfast settle in the water, I heard Ferdinand call out to me. I didn't answer.

'Are you in here?' Ferdinand screeched from the bathroom door.

'Yes,' I groaned.

'Oh. Not well? Morning sickness?' he snickered.

I heard the door close, pushed myself up off the floor, pressed the button to flush the contents, and made my way to the washbasin. I didn't look in the mirror, but splashed cold water on my face and washed my hands. 'Now what?'

'You are in early today,' Ferdinand said, while he made himself a short black. 'Thanks for putting on the coffee machine. You don't look so good. Hope it's not contagious.'

I didn't know how to respond. Technically, my upset stomach wasn't contagious, but he will no doubt feel quite sick when he's charged. 'I ate too much last night. All good.'

He frowned the frown he saved for me when he didn't believe me, or was waiting for me to demand something.

'I've got some calls to make, so I'm shutting my office door.'

Sitting at my desk in the direct line of sight of Ferdinand made the skin on the back of my neck prickle. But I had to be "normal", whatever that was.

'What will happen now?' I asked my uncle when he answered his phone.

'Don't let on, don't say anything. He can't suspect we are on to him. Leave it all to the police and other specialists. Can you do that?'

I wanted to scream into the phone that he asked the impossible. I couldn't pretend everything was ok when he told me it wasn't. Instead, I told him I would try my best.

Ferdinand opened my office door just as I put my mobile on the desk. I jumped.

'Goodness. If you are that sick, why don't you go home?'

It was a good question. There wasn't any reason for me to be in the office. I could work from home, like I did sometimes during COVID. But working from home would be pointless. I would worry about what he was doing.

'Thank you for thinking of me, Ferdinand. But Sherryn will distract me if I go home, and I won't get any work done.'

'Suit yourself. Just make up your mind which Brad you are, will you? Today you are the new Brad. Yesterday the old one crept back in.'

I nodded and asked him to close the door on his way out. My diary popped up on my screen, and I did my best to concentrate on my clients and their needs.

30

EBONY

Ebony opened the door between the garage and the house; Brad had driven in ten minutes earlier and still not come inside. He was sitting in the car, head resting on his hands; they in turn were on the steering wheel. She turned on the garage light rather than open the driver's door and startle him. She was the one who was startled. He lifted his head off the steering wheel and looked at her. Dry tears stained his cheeks, while new ones formed and followed the path of the others down his face. His eyes were red and puffy.

'Come on. Out of the car.' Ebony lent over and undid Brad's seat belt and stepped back while he put his feet on the concrete floor. His knees buckled, and she grabbed him before he collapsed.

Ebony helped Brad into the house and onto the couch in the family room. She took him a glass of water and two paracetamol tablets. 'Take these. It's all I've got. They should help a little.'

'Help with what?' Brad grizzled. 'Help with the deception of someone I considered family? Help me come to grips with my psychopathic brother?'

'No. They won't help that. Take them anyway.'

Brad swallowed the tablets and handed Ebony the glass. 'Thank you. I'm sorry I snapped.'

'I understand. You should go upstairs and try to sleep a bit. I'll bring something up for you to eat later.'

'Can I stay here on the couch? I don't want to be on my own.'

Ebony took a pillow from the linen closet, helped Brad take off his shoes, and when he lay down, covered him with the throw rug. 'The first thing to do when trying to have a nap is to close your eyes,' she said, pulling the rug up under his chin. 'I'll organise some dinner, but I will be quiet.'

From where she worked in the kitchen, Ebony could not tell if Brad was sleeping or lying still with his eyes closed. Either way, he needed the time to take stock of what had happened in his life, and to work out where to from here.

Ebony put the finishing touches on the vegetable stir-fry she had in the wok, took it off the stove, and set out two plates. She knew Brad well and expected him to sit up when the smell wafted into the family room. He didn't. She walked over to the couch and, although it was clear he had been crying before nodding off, he was now asleep. While she was deciding whether she should eat or wait for him to wake up, he called out that dinner smelt great.

'I thought you were sound asleep,' Ebony said from the kitchen.

'I was. But the smell of whatever it is you have going on over there, woke me up.'

Ebony told Brad to stay on the couch and she took over a plate with stir fry and noodles on a tray. She sat next to him.

'You are breaking the rules,' Brad said, as he put

his fork into the vegetables. 'We are not allowed to eat here. That is why we have a dining table.'

'Smart-arse. This is the one exception.' Ebony eyes followed as Brad took small mouthfuls of what was usually one of his favourite dinners. His state of mind worried her.

'I'm ok,' he said, as if reading her thoughts. 'I haven't shed tears like this since Mum died. I'm feeling very sorry for myself, and when I get over my self-pity, I'll be able to move on.'

'I think you are entitled to self-pity. You don't have to eat it all if you are not up to it.'

'Thanks. Think I'll have a shower. The stir fry is great. I'll have the rest tomorrow.'

Ebony stood by as Brad struggle up the stairs. When he was out of sight, she picked up his phone, scrolled through the contacts, and called his Uncle Walton.

'Hello, Brad.'

'It's not Brad, Walton, it's Sherryn. Brad's partner.'

'Is Brad ok?'

'Not really. That's why I'm calling. I've never seen him like this. He's shattered, heartbroken by Ferdinand's betrayal. What can you tell me about what happens next?'

'The police will probably have questions for Brad when they work through their investigation. The Fraud and Extortion Squad of Victoria Police has the comprehensive report compiled by the forensic accountants and auditors I engaged to look into the trust fund. Based on that report, they went to Ferdinand's apartment this evening and charged him. They have refused him bail and he will remain in custody while the investigation progresses. There is nothing for you or Brad to worry about.'

'Hmm. I don't think Brad would agree. What about Steven? Do you know anything about him?'

'You should speak to Sandy and his friend at Vic-Pol. I'm not privy to that situation.'

'Thank you for your time, Walton.'

'Certainly, Sherryn. Let me know if I can help further.'

Ebony put Brad's uneaten dinner in a container and into the fridge. She cleaned up the kitchen and used her phone to call Sandy.

'Hi. How's Brad?'

'Not good. He's having a shower. He didn't eat his dinner. He's very upset. I've never seen him like this.'

'I'm not surprised. Ferdinand was his right-hand man. He trusted him with everything to do with the business, and even personal things.'

'Do you know why he took the money from the Trust Fund?'

'No. But Brad's uncle thinks his assistant Phillip is the connection. Phillip would never leave Walton's employ. Ferdinand could have been building a nest egg to lure Phillip away from Macedon.'

'Words fail me, Sandy. Thanks for your help. Talk soon.' Ebony put her phone on the coffee table, and jumped when Brad spoke from behind.

'What did Sandy have to add?'

'Only that your uncle thinks Ferdinand might have tried to lure Phillip to him with the promise of access to lots of money. But Phillip would never leave your uncle.'

'Is Uncle Walton sure of that? I was absolutely rock

solid sure that Ferdinand was more trustworthy than anyone else in my life. Even you.'

'I hope you have changed your mind about me.'

'I hope so, too. Thanks for dinner, and for putting up with me. Is it ok with you if I go to my place? I need some alone time. I need to process and plan.'

'I'd rather you stayed here.' Ebony put her hands on either side of Brad's face and tilted his head so he was looking at her. 'I will worry more about you if you are not here. I won't bother you. You can sleep down here if you want.'

Brad took Ebony's hands away from his face, kissed her on the forehead, and agreed to stay. They moved towards the couch and together converted it into the double bed it could be.

31

BRAD

I left Ebony a note, saying I was going to my townhouse to have a shower and get ready for work. I appreciated the effort she went to the night before, but I really wanted some time on my own, time to process Ferdinand's deception and betrayal, and time to work out the depth of the embezzlement of funds by Steven in Sapphire Publishing.

Sandy was waiting for me outside my office door. He didn't speak. He stood aside while I unlocked the door and keyed in the alarm code. When we were both inside, he gave me the *don't lie to me* look and walked into the kitchen. I could hear the kettle boiling. 'Don't make me an instant coffee. I couldn't face it.'

'Good to see you are still precious about unimportant stuff,' Sandy grunted, while he made real coffee.

He sat on the other side of my desk while I plugged in the laptop to the large monitor and opened my briefcase. 'Thank you for the coffee,' I said. 'Why here so early?'

'We'll finish our coffee. You will put the laptop to sleep, and we will go to Spencer Street to see Tomy.

ASIC (*Australian Securities and Investments Commission*) has started an investigation into Steven's misappropriation of Sapphire Publishing's funds.'

I didn't cry. There weren't any tears left. They accumulated all day yesterday and found a release on my way to Ebony's last night. A few stragglers appeared when I was lying on the couch in her living room. I leant back in my chair and drank my coffee, looking over the rim of the cup at my friend. 'I don't want to go. I have too much to work out here. To find out if Ferdinand helped himself to any of their money, I need to look into all of my clients' books. Won't ASIC call on me if they want to speak to me?'

'Yes. But Tomy thought you might like a heads up.'

'I don't need a heads up, Sandy. Thank her for me. If any of them need to speak to me, they know where I am. My brother was truthful about our mother, but an embezzling, manipulative psychopath in every other dealing I had with him. I hope he rots. I hope Ferdinand rots too. Oh, and not forgetting Sophie Marris; she can rot alongside them both. Whatever happens to Steven will not bring my father back, and all the guilt that has eaten at me for the last year refuses to leave me in peace. I have to come to terms with my lot.'

'I understand,' Sandy said sagely. 'But when you have finished working through your clients' files, you might want to call your uncle. Phillip has disappeared.'

Phillip's disappearance didn't register as important, but Ebony not answering her phone, did. Panic set in after I tried to reach her for two hours after Sandy left. The old Brad came to the surface so I could cope with my life. The Brad who was resilient, who could build a wall of self-protection and not let any part of it crumble, needed to take over.

I went through all the motions to secure the office after I had unplugged Ferdinand's laptop from the monitor and keyboard. A question of the password popped into my brain for half a second as I put the laptop in my bag. While I was waiting for the elevator, I called Ebony again. I'd tried to get a response for hours, telling myself her phone's battery was flat, she was taking a bath, in the shower, gone for a walk and left the phone at home, had it with her but on silent. All the reasonable scenarios that would make sense to a person in a rational state of mind. I was not. I would have risked speeding fines on the way to the townhouse in Altona if I'd been able to drive at over sixty kilometres an hour in the god awful traffic. I pulled up out the front of the townhouse eight hours after Sandy left my office, and four hours since I'd started calling Ebony. There were no lights on.

Unlocking the door and stepping into the hallway, I noticed the alarm hadn't been set. She must be home. 'Ebony, where are you?' Silence. My heart thumped in my chest like the drum in a marching band. Taking deep breaths and telling myself to calm down, I walked into the kitchen — family room area and turned on the lights. The curtains were open. The kitchen was spotless: no smell of food having been recently prepared or cooked, not even a cup in the sink. I galloped up the stairs, missing every second step. 'Ebony!' I yelled, the frantic tone of my voice bouncing around in the bedroom.

The curtains were open here, too. The bed looked as if it had been made by the housekeeper in a five-star hotel. The ensuite cupboards and drawers were empty. I opened the wardrobe doors and fell to my knees, holding my head in my hands. My few pairs of pants and a couple of shirts were the only things there. Ebony's life had been removed from the Altona townhouse.

EPILOGUE

Sandy banged on the front door. Brad opened it and fell into his friend's arms.

'She's gone.'

'You said that on the phone. I don't understand.'

'What's not to understand? I came here and she's gone. She's not answering her phone. All her things are gone.'

Sandy followed Brad into the family room, and looked at the kitchen. 'Spotless. Looks like no one lives here.'

'No one does.' Brad thumped his body down into an armchair. 'I don't get it. She was caring, loving, supportive when I got here yesterday.'

'I know, she called me, all concerned for your welfare. There has to be an explanation. I'll look around for signs of a struggle.'

While Brad waited for Sandy to finish his search, he dialled Ebony's number again. This time, the response from Telstra was that the number had been disconnected. He threw his phone across the floor.

'What happened?' Sandy bounded down the stairs.

'She has had her number disconnected. That's it. We're done. Did you find anything?'

'No. It's as you said, everything was removed carefully. Nothing left behind. Let's go. It's not good for you to be here. Come back to my place.'

Brad collected his phone off the floor, closed the curtains and blinds in the family room and kitchen and keyed in the alarm as he and Sandy left.

'Do you want to get drunk?' Sandy asked, when he and Brad were in his kitchen, sitting at the bench.

'I don't think so. I need a clear head.'

Sandy pulled random menus out of one of the kitchen drawers. 'What do you feel like eating?'

'I don't.'

'Tough titties. You are going to eat something. I'll order Chinese.'

While Sandy put his phone to his ear to order the food, Brad moved outside onto Sandy's small alfresco area. The sun was setting, and the mozzies would be out for blood soon, but he craved fresh air.

'Do you want to eat out here?' Sandy asked. 'Food will be twenty minutes.'

'If you have insect repellent we could eat out here. That would be nice.'

'Done.'

As promised, the food arrived in just over twenty minutes, and the friends shared the contents of four different courses, taking their plates outside.

'Your phone is ringing,' Sandy said, through a mouthful of vegetarian fried rice.

'It's Uncle Walton.' Brad didn't answer the call.

The Betrayal of Ebony Makepeace

'Now *my* phone is ringing,' Sandy groaned. 'It's your uncle. Hello, Mr Warburton.'

'Hello, Mr Sanderson. Is my nephew with you? I've called a few times. He isn't answering.'

'His phone is on the blink. He's here with me. I'll get him.'

Brad mouthed "no, no, no", but Sandy passed him the phone.

'Uncle Walton. What's up?'

'I'm in Melbourne. Where are you? I must see you now.'

'I'm at Sandy's. He will text you the address.'

Sandy showed Walton into the family room, where Brad was curled up in a chair, and offered him a glass of wine.

'No thank you. I know you two are very close, but I have something to say that you might not want anyone else to know, Brad.'

'There is nothing you can say to me that my best friend, my real brother, over there, shouldn't know too. Go for it.'

'The police have come to a different conclusion from the one we formed about Ferdinand and the money in the Minors Trust.' Walton waited for his nephew to absorb the information.

'Ok. And?' Brad sat up straight in the chair.

'They have released Ferdinand pending further enquiries. Phillip and your Miss Forbes are the prime suspects.'

To be continued in Book 3, *The Revenge of Ebony Makepeace*.

ABOUT THE AUTHOR

Janeen Ann O'Connell was born and grew up in Melbourne, Victoria, Australia. Her parents separated before her first birthday, and her maternal grandmother had primary care of Janeen until she was six. It was her grandmother's strong sense of justice, her strong political will, and the passion filled stories she told of her childhood and the Depression years, that instilled a love of family history and politics into the aspiring writer. It was during her family history research that Janeen learned her grandmother's cousin was Premier of the State of Victoria from 1924 until 1927 and her uncle was a mayor and councillor in regional Victoria. Janeen now understood where her interest in politics came from.

Her family history has lots more secrets, adventures, political misadventures, pioneer challenges, insane asylum admissions, bankruptcies and happy stories to share. Janeen lives in a suburb of Melbourne, Victoria, Australia with her husband and their miniature poodle, Teddy. She has two daughters, one son, four granddaughters and one grandson.

To learn more about Janeen Ann O'Connell and discover more Next Chapter authors, visit our website at www.nextchapter.pub.

The Betrayal of Ebony Makepeace
ISBN: 978-4-82415-612-9
Mass Market

Published by
Next Chapter
2-5-6 SANNO
SANNO BRIDGE
143-0023 Ota-Ku, Tokyo
+818035793528

8th November 2022

www.ingramcontent.com/pod-product-compliance
Lightning Source LLC
LaVergne TN
LVHW032010070526
838202LV00059B/6376